Shire Summer

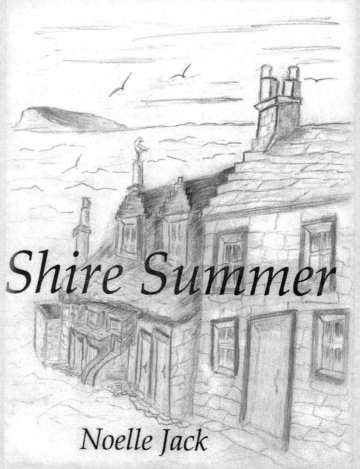

Shire Summer

Noelle Jack

ARCHWAY
PUBLISHING

Archway Publishing books may be ordered
through booksellers or by contacting:

Archway Publishing
1663 Liberty Drive
Bloomington, IN 47403
www.archwaypublishing.com
1 (888) 242-5904

Because of the dynamic nature of the Internet, any web
addresses or links contained in this book may have changed
since publication and may no longer be valid. The views
expressed in this work are solely those of the author and do
not necessarily reflect the views of the publisher, and the
publisher hereby disclaims any responsibility for them.

Any people depicted in stock imagery provided by Thinkstock are
models, and such images are being used for illustrative purposes only.
Certain stock imagery © Thinkstock.

ISBN: 978-1-4808-2275-7 (sc)
ISBN: 978-1-4808-2276-4 (e)

Library of Congress Control Number: 2015915996

Print information available on the last page.

Archway Publishing rev. date: 11/16/2015

To my husband, Roderick,
for his unfailing encouragement and support

*"And now we reach…the very sanctuary of the East Wind.
The great rocks…look as if they had been cracked and split
by the great hammer of Thor before the sea began to wear
them smooth. Every jutting point has its cap of white, and
from every hollow comes a murmur of waves. The breeze prowls,
keen and unsatisfied…over the braes and round the boulders…"*

John Geddie   <u>The Fringes of Fife</u>

*Whenever the moon and stars are set,
Whenever the wind is high,
All night long in the dark and wet,
A man goes riding by.
Late in the night when the fires are out,
Why does he gallop and gallop about?
Whenever the trees are crying aloud,
And ships are tossed at sea,
By, on the highway, low and loud,
By at the gallop goes he.
By at the gallop he goes, and then
By he comes back at the gallop again.*

Robert Louis Stevenson   <u>A Child's Garden of Verses</u>

The pencil drawing on the title page is the author's rendering of an ink sketch by June Johnston from <u>Fringes of Fife</u>. With permission of Lang Syne Publishers Ltd., Newtongrange, Midlothian

Though many names are changed, the characters and places in this work of fiction are based on real people and locations.

Contents

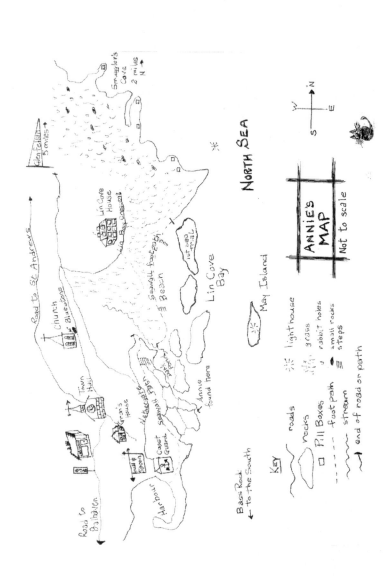

Prologue

It was the sirens Annie thought she remembered and the drone of planes in the night. She thought she stood in the garden then, because she remembered the searchlights making long silver pathways in the dark sky above her house.

"You were far too young," her mother said.

"But I heard them, Mummy, and saw things too, I'm sure I did."

"At night when the bombers came we were inside, darling, with the blackout curtains drawn tight across each window."

"Oh."

*   *   *

A man came home at intervals, in uniform. He set his huge kit bag on the floor in the hall, pulled the cap with the gold crest from his head and threw his arms around her mother.

"Give your Daddy a big hug, darling." She turned to the small girl who stood watching. "He loves you too, you know."

Annie shrank back. She did not know this man with the crooked smile and tears in his eyes.

*   *   *

Along the beach, where the surf pounded in and the gulls wailed, there were great rolls of barbed wire. Annie wanted to run into the waves but the wire was everywhere.

"Never, ever go near there. There are mines buried in the sand. They could explode at any time."

But sometimes the village boys went close; once on stilts she remembers. They laughed and pointed with their long wooden legs pretending they were guns, "POW! POW! POW! POW!" They didn't look scared at all.

And Annie saw the fishing boats on the water far from shore. They were out in every kind of weather.

"How can they get back in? Will the mines blow up under them too?"

"Of course not."

It was all a long time ago.

* * *

But what Annie knows now about the war is how it lingers even though it's over and her father's home for good this time.

The sheep that wander in the fields above the beach now find shelter from the wind inside the concrete pill boxes where the guns once sat. Annie has seen the circle of slits from their tomb-like insides. She has peered through dark angled openings at the grey seas beyond.

And there are rabbits everywhere, and rabbit holes you don't see till your foot catches in one. The bunnies are fast but not always lucky. People set snares for them since other meats are rationed. Annie eats a lot of rabbit stew.

And there are tins of dried 'tigers' milk in the kitchen cupboard and boxes of powdered eggs; butter's just for Sunday breakfast, and chocolate, on those rare occasions when it's in the shops, requires a ration book.

*   *   *

...and everything now is because of then.

Chapter One

Balhaven

"Hey, Annie!" Elspeth yelled, racing from the stone archway across the school quadrangle. "I've got it! I've got it!" She waved a large royal blue book in both hands over her head, her school bag thumping against her back, her hat askew.

Annie turned from a gaggle of uniformed girl-friends in brown tunics, striped ties and blazers and broke into a grin. "Slow down, Else, I hear you!"

"I told you I'd get it," said Elspeth puffing from exertion.

"Fantabulous! Your sister *actually* let you have her precious yearbook?"

Elspeth nodded still breathless, "But not without a fight." She yanked on Annie's arm.

"Oops, 'scuse us; see you chaps later," Annie said with a laugh. She hopped on one foot for balance and reached for her bag. "So you had to beat it out of her?"

"Nah, just a lot of promises." Elspeth linked arms

with her taller schoolmate and pulled her out of earshot.

"So, Else, what *do* you owe her?"

"Kitchen duty, plus making her bed for a whole week."

"Poor you. She's tough, Emma is."

"And with *conditions*. I have to give it back without even the teensiest mark before supper tonight. She'll probably even check it for fingerprints!"

"With her spy kit!" Annie joked.

"That'd be Emma!"Elspeth shot back.

"Come *on* then, stop wasting time. Let's have a look." From force of habit Annie brushed away the long braids she no longer had and tucked her bobbed chestnut hair behind her ears instead; a useless effort because it fell in her eyes anyway when she leaned in closer.

"Not here, Annie; I don't want everyone hanging around; let's go to our place."

The girls marched in step over the cobblestones to a quiet corner where the high wall surrounding the schoolyard had been stripped of its ivy greenery. They dropped their school bags, blazers and hats and scrunched down. Leaning against the rough, sun warmed stone they stared at their prize. The cover of Emma's book was of royal blue leather, "St. Andrew's Academy" emblazoned in gold letters across it.

"Wow!" Annie breathed. "Even the binding gives me the shivers."

With a sweep of her arms Elspeth opened the yearbook somewhere near the middle. The spine crackled. Annie crowded closer.

"You're skipping pages, Else."

"Wait," she flipped back a few. "So, what'd'ya think of *that*?" Else had opened the album to a full-page spread of a spacious building with a glass roof.

"Is that a *swimming* pool?"Annie sputtered.

"*St. Andrew's latest addition to the sports program,*" Else read, grinning like the proverbial Cheshire cat.

"That's fantabulous!" Annie threw her fist in the air. "Maybe I'll *finally* be able to perfect my crawl. It's the breathing that's murder, you know."

"No flies on you. I'm still struggling with my breaststroke!"

"Then we'll practice together, Else; one length at a time."

Elspeth flipped a few more pages.

There was page after page of class pictures with serious- looking students in gowns and mortar boards. There were photographs of playing fields and running tracks and buildings with arched windows and towers. It was like a playground full of castles.

"Wow! Is that the choir?" This picture had been taken inside a chapel, by the looks of it. Annie twisted her neck to get a better look. "Else, can I hold the book a minute?"

"Okay, but careful; clean fingers, right?"

Annie licked a few and rubbed them on her tunic. "There; how's that?" She pulled the book into her lap before Else could say more.

There were stained glass windows in the photo-graph and an organ with rows of pipes rising upward. "I bet they do part singing. I *adore* harmony, Else. I get goose bumps hearing all the notes mix together."

"I don't care about the singing so much; I just want to be in the drama club. Emma says they might do "*Annie Get Your Gun*" next year."

"That's got plenty of singing."

"And other acting stuff, right?" Else looked hopeful.

"I know all the songs from the picture. I've seen it five times at least!"

"You could audition for 'Annie', Annie!" Else laughed.

"*Doin' what comes naturally!*" Annie burst into song. "You know that one?"

Else looked blank.

"Oh, wow, Else, I'm in love with "St. Andrew's" already.

"Come on, Annie; *turn*; there's lots more to see."

She turned.

"Hey wait a sec! I missed this bit last time." Elspeth started reading over Annie's shoulder.

"*Members of the "St. Andrew's Academy Outdoors Club" spent the May holiday weekend hiking, climbing, and paddling in the Loch Katrine district. Sleeping in tents and cooking over campfires gave the students plenty of experience in roughing it.*"

"We would be the 'Ladies of the Lake'!" Annie swooned, reciting her favorite lines from the famous poem by Sir Walter Scott.

'*The silver light, with quivering glance,*
Played on the water's still expanse'

"What ladies?" Else's brow furrowed.

"Oh, never mind. But wouldn't it be fantastic to be out in a canoe? Can't you just see us dipping our paddles and skimming over the lake? If we're in the same class again we'd be there together. Oh, Else..."said Annie drifting off into her own world again.

"*If* they keep us Balhaven girls together." Elspeth announced with some force tracing a pattern on the flagstones with her finger. She looked up suddenly. "They will, won't they? It would be awful to have *all* new people in your class."

"Yeah, it would. I'd hate to be the only Bal' girl in the room. I'd feel so *conspicuous.*"

"Oh, speaking of being together or not, I probably won't see you so much this summer."

Annie frowned. "Why's that?"

"My parents have decided on that France holiday after all. Not my first choice. We'll be gone most of July, staying with cousins in Normandy."

"Oh," Annie forced a smile. "I think you did say something a while back."

"I may have to speak French," Else added looking worried.

"You'll be fine. You're top of the class in that subject."Annie paused, her smile fading. "Oh, but I *am* going to miss you Else."

"Me too, but it is just a few weeks." She brushed some dust off her hat. "So, you finished planning our next term?"

"You want it back already? I've only just started." Annie said, chagrined.

"We've got it for the rest of the day, silly." Elspeth reached for the book and snapped it closed. She eased it protectively in her satchel then got to her feet.

"You know, Else, I'm going to be sorry to leave this old place."Annie said as she picked up her stuff.

"Me too. We've had some terrific times here. Remember the Christmas Concert when just about everyone had chicken pox?"

"And you had to sing the descant in 'Silent Night' at the last minute?"

"And I had to do that highland dance in Carol's place?"

"And we were both s-o-o hopeless?"

"But we didn't have any spots!"

"And then they used Colin to play Mary because he had 'such a sweet voice'?"

"And his veil fell off and he had some old tweed cap on his head?"

Both girls collapsed with laughter and sat down on the pavement again to catch their breath. Else recovered first, and with a grin, looked to the top of the wall above them. "You remember when we climbed up there last year? Using that poor old vine? Oh, boy did we get into trouble!"

"Do I! Even Miss Sinclair shouted over that."

They had walked for several wild minutes along the top of the sea wall that protected the east side of the school grounds. The wind had whipped at their hair and when they dared to look down they saw the waves pounding on the rocks sending up showers of salty spray. It had been unbelievably exciting until the shouting started.

"And Miss S. never shouts."

"And Miss Evans said she might even *expel* us!"

Elspeth stood up and slipped her arms through the straps of her satchel. "And poor old Mr. Birrell; he just loved that old ivy and Evans made him cut down every last leaf and twig of it. *"We can't have students climbing up there and plunging to their deaths on the rocks,"* Elspeth imitated the Head's stern voice then teetered on tiptoe pretending to fall.

"As if they would; the wall's wide as anything." Annie copied Elspeth, her arms stretched out.

"Elspeth Rankin," said a smartly dressed woman who appeared from the other side of a dissolving game of chase, "you're not thinking of having another go at that wall, are you?"

"Oh, no, Miss Sinclair."

Miss Sinclair was their home form teacher; Annie adored her. She loved the way Miss S. put on different voices when she read aloud and told them juicy stories about kings and queens too. It was as though she had read their diaries.

"And what about you, Annie McLeod?"

"Absolutely not, Miss Sinclair."

"Glad to hear it."

They were still having giggling fits when nine loud chimes echoed across the playground. A cloud of crows flew up from the clock tower, flapping and squawking. By the time they had drifted back on their turret perches the girls had joined the surge of uniformed students trooping through the open door of the school.

Chapter Two

A House by the Sea

Annie ran most of the way home from the bus stop bubbling with stories to share about the glories of "St. Andrew's". She hoped her mother would have time to listen but she could never be sure now since all the changes.

She skidded to a stop outside her house and took in the newly painted sign that read: LIN COVE GUEST HOUSE. What was the summer going to be like now with hotel visitors everywhere? Her mother was unspeakably busy; her father too, pitching in whenever he could between his Coast Guard duties and his studies. For a fact there wouldn't be any caravan holiday *this* year.

She burst through the kitchen door, all enthusiasm and hope anyway and flung her arms around her mother's waist. "I'm home! And guess what? Elspeth got Emma's book and..."

"Not now, love. I'm right in the middle of a new recipe and I have to concentrate."

"But you should have seen the "St. Andrew's" book, Mum, it was *gorgeous*."

"Annie, please."

"Okay, *I know.* Later right?" She knew it wouldn't be soon enough.

"I'm sorry, dear, but this is very important." Her mother's attention went right back to the cook book.

"So I'm *not* important I suppose," Annie whispered to herself. This kind of rejection was getting all too familiar. She grabbed her school bag and stomped off to the small comfort of her new room. Maybe Bozz would be there curled up on her bed. At least a cat would listen.

A few guests sat in the newly furnished lounge as Annie crossed it to reach the stairs. Some were reading, others were writing post cards or staring out the windows at the sea view. Their presence made *her* feel watched. They were invading her privacy and, in her opinion, a home should be private.

* * *

The kitchen counters were still stacked with dirty dishes when Annie came down for supper and there was no sign of the kitchen staff either. Aileen and Molly must have gone home. To add to the strangeness her parents, who had clearly finished eating, were sitting there in silence over their empty plates. Were they waiting for her? But why? They hardly ever ate together anymore. Meals were a 'fit them in on the fly' affair since the hotel opened; eaten between cooking and serving guests or other obligations so that Annie felt no need to follow a schedule either.

"Ah, Annie, you're here." Her mother rose.

Now that was odd too, her mother getting up for her like that.

"I can help myself, mummy. Plate's in the oven, right?" She pulled open the door of the huge gas oven and took out her portion of some sort of stew and vegetables. It smelled good.

"We have to talk," said her mother after Annie pulled up her chair.

"What about, Mummy?" She picked up her fork then put it down again. Their silence was a shade too long.

Her father cleared his throat and poured water in his glass. A little of it spilled on the table. He dabbed at it with his napkin. "We have some difficult news."

"Oh?" Annie was getting the jitters.

"We thought it best not to tell you any sooner than necessary," her mother added, "but obviously we can't wait any longer."

"What's wrong, Mummy?" Annie pressed her hands against the table edge and leaned in. "You're not ill, are you?"

She shook her head. "Oh no, nothing like that. I'm fine, dear. It's just that... That your father and I have had a long talk and we realize we can't..."

"You're not going to like this," her father interrupted, "though you probably have your suspicions with all the changes that have gone on."

"You mean about the hotel, don't you?" It wasn't really a question.

"For the most part, yes," he said.

"I suppose it's to make more money because you're not working right now, Daddy." Annie looked vaguely round the remodeled kitchen with its long counters and deep sinks; it was like something a restaurant might have, not a home. "But it must have cost heaps to do all this, didn't it?"

"It did," her mother agreed. "And we thought that the sale of Grandpa Mac's estate would pay for the renovations and leave money to spare, but..." she didn't finish.

"So what happened?"

"We had a nasty shock a few weeks back. The government informed us that there were some hefty back taxes owing on his property."

"This is too much information for her, Margaret."

"No it isn't, Daddy. I want to know."

Her mother sighed. "So suddenly there is very *little* money in our account. We are not poor but we can't spend more than this hotel can earn for us and that is only just starting to happen."

Her father cleared his throat. "But in the end we should be ahead. The hotel should pay for itself in two or three years and provide us with a solid income. By then I should be working too. But in the meantime, we need to cut some corners."

"Corners?" Annie's eyebrows lifted.

"Your school fees, honey," her dad said twisting his water glass. "We simply can't afford the extravagance of a private boarding school."

Annie poked at her mashed potatoes with her fork. "I don't understand."

Her mother's face creased with concern. "What we're trying to tell you, dearest, is that "St. Andrew's", next term, is quite out of the question."

Annie dared not reply. It would make it true if she did. The ticking of the kitchen clock seemed suddenly louder. The sun flickered through the curtains making patterns on the wall.

"Of course the other part of the problem," her father was saying as though from a distance, "is that I haven't brought in much money since leaving the Navy."

Annie forced herself to speak. "So why didn't you stay, Daddy?"

"Ask your mother."

"Because *I* didn't want him to," Margaret McLeod said reaching for her husband's hand. "You were away so much, Sandy. I was honestly glad when you decided to leave and go back to school."

His face had a faraway look. "But I couldn't give up the sea completely."

Annie knew that. "So that's why you work for the Coast Guard, Daddy, isn't it?"

"And because it's just part time."

"So why not work there full time?" Annie wasn't used to challenging her father. She shifted awkwardly in her chair.

"Because we have *all this* to manage," his gaze took in the room around them. *"And* there's my degree. It takes a long time when you can only study in the evenings."

Annie could see that.

"Once Daddy is qualified as a naval architect it will be a huge step forward; for all of us," her mother explained.

"We just have to be patient," her father continued. But he didn't look patient, he looked cross. "And being in this house, with paying summer visitors, goes a long way to solving our money problems."

"So, that's it. That's the story." Her mother let out a long breath and waited for Annie to speak.

"Then not going on to "St. Andrew's"; you really mean it, don't you?"

Her father leaned toward her but Annie shrank back. He waited a moment, studying her face then went on. "We do, honey; funds just aren't there for an expensive school and especially now after this latest setback."

Annie's mind was spinning trying to think of something to change their minds. Desperate to make a difference she said, "Well then, maybe I don't need to board like the others. Could you afford just the day school?" Her heart sank as she made the offer. Boarding was going to be such a huge part of it all.

"Sandy, tell her how very difficult this is for us too, please!"

He shook his head then spoke gently. "There's no point fighting this, honey. The sooner you can face what we're saying the easier it will be for everyone."

"But I don't want to face it! It's too awful. My friends; they'll all be there and I won't!" She struggled with tears.

"We know it's going to be hard, darling," her father said. "We know that, we really do."

"Hard! It's going to be *unbearable!*" Annie pushed her untouched meal aside.

"Tomorrow will be your last day at "Balhaven" anyway, my love," said her mother looking genuinely upset, "and by the end of summer perhaps it won't seem so bad." She glanced at her daughter's plate. "Won't you try to eat *something* at least?"

Annie shook her head. Her parents had their minds made up for some time, apparently, so there really *was* no point in dragging it out.

"Excuse me," she said mustering her last ounce of self-control, "I'm going up to my room. Sorry." Annie shoved her chair back and ran out into the hall and up the stairs.

*   *   *

"Such a rush you're in, my dear," said an elderly guest on the first floor landing. "It's Annie, isn't it?" the visitor pressed.

But Annie shot up the last flight of stairs without answering. How she hated the way total strangers could spy on her feelings!

Bozz, padded after her.

Chapter Three

Too Many Goodbyes

From the window of the wheezing, petrol-smelly, Bluewing bus Annie caught glimpses of the July sunshine glistening on the sea. The "old bird" rolled up and down the hilly coast road through centuries-old villages of aged stone houses and tall-spired churches.

Annie was feeling ill. It wasn't just the petrol, it was the fact that she hadn't slept most of the night before. Her head pounded from tiredness and her eyes were puffy from tears. She had dawdled purposely on the way to the bus so she'd miss the regular one her friends caught. But now even this one barreled relentlessly along the coast road to "Balhaven". Fields of mounded yellow blossoms shone like sunlight against the rich brown earth and the early summer barley swayed in mint green waves. Annie's eyes prickled. How could it all be so beautiful out there when her life was so awful?

If she didn't go on to "St. Andrew's" her friends would be gone. They'd drift away like gulls over the ocean. It had happened just like that after Linda moved. She'd promised to write; that a new school wouldn't change anything, but it did. It wasn't anyone's fault; it just happened.

And then there was that other thing to deal with too; the fact that her parents *couldn't afford* to send her to a fancy school any more.

"I can't look them in the eye and say that; I just can't," Annie whispered to the empty seat beside her.

*   *   *

Annie had timed her arrival at school perfectly because the last chime had already sounded when she reached the archway. She wouldn't need to speak to anyone now, including Elspeth. Annie ran to join the last stragglers into class.

All morning she kept her head down, staring at her books or scribbling furiously in her notebooks.

"P-s-s-s-t, Annie," Elspeth whispered across the aisle in Miss Morgan's math class. This lesson was as dull as usual but Annie kept her eyes glued to the blackboard as though fascinated with the review of the last term's work.

Elspeth tried again, more loudly. "P-s-s-s-t; at least *look* at me."

Annie ignored the plea and made her fingers copy numbers while her fuzzy brain planned her next escape from Elspeth.

*   *   *

In the final morning class Annie excused herself ahead of the bell and hid in one of the bathroom cubicles in order to give her usual crowd time to get seated for lunch. Reaching the dining hall door some ten minutes later she hesitated for a moment then took a deep breath and marched in. She ignored Elspeth's immediate and frantic wave. When Elspeth made a move to stand up Carol grabbed her sleeve and yanked her back down. Annie couldn't hear what Carol said but she could guess. She didn't dare to check and see if Elspeth looked back again.

Annie moved to an empty table a few seats down from one of the least popular girls in the school and hoped there would be no reason to talk. It didn't work.

"What are *you* doing this summer, Annie?" asked Heather after an awkward silence. She had pushed aside the book she was reading.

Annie didn't answer; her voice would shake for certain.

When this led nowhere Heather soldiered on, "My father is going to Venezuela on business. He's taking Harry and me with him."

Lovely, thought Annie; Heather's in Venezuela, Elspeth's in France and I'm stuck in my little attic!

But Heather just wasn't going to give up. "My father says it will broaden our horizons."

Annie cleared her throat, "I suppose so," she managed and looked over her shoulder expecting that at any second Elspeth would bear down on her demanding explanations. For something to do she unwrapped her sandwich.

"I didn't even know where Venezuela was,"

Heather said giving it her best shot, "so I got this from the library, see." She pushed a book across the table.

Annie flipped over a couple of pages then pushed the book back. "I hope you have a wonderful time."

"Me too."

The two girls sat without speaking after that. The hands on the dining hall clock crawled through the lunch time hour. Whenever Annie took a bite from the edge of her sandwich she glanced at Heather, willing her not to speak again.

"That's Elspeth over there, isn't it?" said Heather pointing. "She's been staring at us all through lunch."

Annie stood. "Sorry, Heather, I have to go."

"That's okay."

Annie tossed her lunch, bag and all, into the waste basket.

*   *   *

The afternoon was a miserable continuation of the morning. Desperate to remain invisible Annie slipped between the double row of cabinets near the science room door when the class filed in. She stayed there for the entire lesson, gazing at the peculiar bottled specimens that lined the shelves; the grey lumps in greenish liquid with the unreadable labels. When she rejoined her class after the bell rang no one seemed to have noticed her absence.

Nice, I've gone already as far as they are concerned, Annie told herself. But in a way it was a relief; it made the goodbyes easier.

Miss Sinclair's class was the last. Annie dreaded

that her teacher would talk about "St. Andrew's" but she didn't. The head mistress must have said something. How like Miss Sinclair to keep silent for her sake. She could have given the girls a real pep talk on what they would be getting into as they moved up but she never referred to it once. But after all the students had straggled out, miraculously including Elspeth, Miss Sinclair came over to her. Annie was taking the last things from her desk.

"Annie, I'm so sorry," she said settling into an adjoining chair.

Annie pushed a dog eared copy of Prince Caspian into her schoolbag. It had the name 'Elspeth' in red ink on the cover.

"I know how much you were looking forward to moving on with the others. It must be very difficult now to find out otherwise; to have all this change to deal with so suddenly and…and… not to be with them all, that is."

It was odd to hear her teacher struggle with words but Annie couldn't think of a thing to say to make the conversation easier.

"You are a strong girl, Annie, a good friend and a good student," Miss Sinclair continued, regaining her teacherly composure, "and I believe you will do well no matter what school you find yourself in." Her kind eyes and warm smile reached out to soothe Annie. "Think about that, won't you?"

"I'll try. Thank you, Miss Sinclair… for everything."Annie swallowed back the lump in her throat, picked up her things and left.

*   *   *

"Come on, sit with us," Carol said walking up to Annie's seat at the back of the bus.

Annie shifted closer to the window cradling her stuffed school bag into her lap. "No thanks, I can't, not now."

"What's wrong? You've not said a word all day to anyone." Carol moved closer and started to sit down.

Annie put her hands up, waving her off. "I'm fine. Just leave me alone, please."

Carol wasn't one to give up easily. "So you're going to sulk all by yourself back here?"

"Yes." Annie couldn't manage another syllable.

Carol waited then shrugged. "Well, if that's really how you want it. Have a nice summer."

Some of the others looked back and waved for Carol to rejoin them. Annie stared through her reflection in the window. So that's it, "St. Andrew's" and now all my friends too have gone up in smoke.

One by one the girls climbed off the bus with waves of goodbye to each other. They set off up driveways toward rambling farms or manor style houses; places where there had been such wonderful parties with cakes and presents, games and country dancing, even magicians sometimes. It hadn't occurred to Annie, until yesterday, that these friends were far better off than her. Would they cut her out entirely now? Would they come and visit her in a home turned into a summer hotel? Not Pygmalion likely!

Oh, why hadn't she been better prepared? Why hadn't she realized that the changes taking place in her home and in her parents' hushed and worried conversations were going to change her life too? Maybe it wouldn't have hurt so much if she had been ready.

The workmen had all gone now, thank goodness, the ones with the power saws that screeched, and the hammers that pounded. Plumbers had yanked pieces out of bedroom walls to install washbasins and electricians had pulled wires. Dust had flown and settled everywhere. Tempers had been short and Annie had longed for it all to be over. And, when it was, she had been turned out of her room and relocated in the attic.

"Just for the season," her mother explained. The view was panoramic but there wasn't enough space under the gabled ceiling for all her stuff. It felt foreign, not hers. *And* there were strangers everywhere; adult strangers. Her parents had decided that mature guests with no children would be easier to accommodate than whole families.

The bus stopped for Annie opposite "Gibson's" where it always did. She clumped down the high steps, head down, and then crossed the cobbled street to stand outside the shop window. There wasn't much of interest there; just stacks of *The Daily Express* newspaper, some *Scots Pictorial* calendars and *The Ladies Home Journal* on a rack. In behind were shelves lined with tins of vegetables, Tiger's milk powder, dried eggs and some uninteresting looking biscuits. The only sweets, if you could call them that, were some bitter licorice sticks or pokes of fizzy sherbet. But it was habit to stop there and habit was soothing in its way. She fingered the coins in her pocket, and pushed open the swinging door. The bell suspended over it jangled.

"Well, if it isn't wee Annie McLeod!" called the old gentleman in the striped apron shuffling out from the back of the shop.

"Some sherbet please, Mr. Gibson; tuppence worth." But the coins slipped from her fingers and rolled across the floor. As she bent to retrieve them her stuffed schoolbag swayed uncomfortably across her back.

"Such a sad face," said Mr. Gibson turning from the overloaded shelves, with a tall glass jar in his hands. He eased it onto the counter and unscrewed the lid. "What could be getting you down on such a fine summer day?"

"It's the last day of school." Annie laid her coins flat on the uneven wooden display case hoping there would be no more questions.

But Mr. Gibson was not to be put off. "Then where are the smiles? No more classes to worry about for weeks, hmm?" He was reaching into the jar again and scooping out more of the colourful packages. "Come now, I'll put in a few extra. How's that?" The pokes rattled into the paper bag.

"Thank you, very much," whispered Annie and fled from the shop setting the doorbell jangling.

Chapter Four

Moira

Annie tossed her school bag on the kitchen floor and pulled off her hat. Her hair stuck out in all directions and her loosened school tie flapped against her untucked blouse. She'd have taken her blazer off to walk home but she hadn't another hand to carry it in. Her face was flushed from exertion.

"You look like something the cat dragged in."

Her mother's remark, when added to a day of hurts, stung. "Thanks," Annie mumbled.

Mrs. McLeod did not react. She just wiped her floury hands on her apron and smiled in Annie's direction looking, for all the world, like something out of one of Mr. Gibson's ladies' magazines. Her smart tartan skirt and lavender blouse was covered by a spotless (apart from the flour) white apron and *her braided* hair was wound expertly across her head. Annie was furious with everything about her including the braids. Why had she ever let her mother cut hers off?

"Tell me about your day, honey. Was it very difficult?" She opened her arms in expectation of the ritual hug.

Annie turned away and didn't answer. How could her mother ask such a question? Difficult? It was nothing but hideous and not something she felt like sharing with the person who had caused it all!

"I can't talk about it now." The reply pleased Annie. It made her sound grown up and in control.

"Well, if that's how you feel, perhaps you had best be off on your own." Mrs. McLeod pulled a handkerchief from her apron pocket and dabbed at her nose. She turned, a bit too quickly Annie thought, and went back to rolling pastry.

Annie had not won that round in the way she had hoped. She had wanted her mother to apologize, to sympathize and ask for Annie's forgiveness and maybe, miraculously, change her mind.

*   *   *

Annie crossed the patch of lawn outside the dining room window, thumped down on the garden swing and rocked back and forth. So, she was on her own, again!

And this certainly wasn't the first time. She'd left piles of friends behind when they'd moved into *this* new house a couple of years ago. *School* was the only place where she got to see any of them. There were the house parties, of course, but now those would probably be over too. To make matters worse there were no kids in the part of the village where they lived, except for

summer visitors. Families would rent the houses on
their street for a couple of weeks during the warm
months; sometimes a girl her age would be among
them but not often and not for long. The rest of the year
they stood empty, staring at the North Sea.

But she would get by. Something would happen.
Her old pal Hamish might show up. They always had
fun together; often dangerous fun that her parents
knew nothing about. And that was just what Annie
felt like now; the more trouble the better. She would
show her parents how rotten she could be if they took
away all the stuff she cared about.

With these thoughts seething away Annie made
her way back into the house ready to cause trouble.

*   *   *

"Back already?" Annie's mother said in greeting.
"Bozz was wondering where you'd got to."

Bozz was her shadow. One was not seen for long
without the other.

"Oh, Bozz," the ebony cat rubbed its face against
Annie's legs, "I would've loved to have you tucked
inside my schoolbag today," she said scooping him up
for a cuddle.

Bozz nuzzled his head into Annie's chin, draping
his legs on either side of her neck. His warm fur and
rumbling purr were the most soothing things that had
happened all day and Annie felt her resentment melt a
little. She looked over Bozz' head at the lemon dessert her
mother was working on. "Is that for the guests or us?"

"There's probably enough for both." She spooned

filling into the waiting tart shells then turned, her smile teasing.

Annie wouldn't smile back.

Her mother put some pans into the sink and wiped off the counter. "Do you feel like talking now, before Molly gets back?"

"Maybe."

"So how *was* your day, honey?"

"Awful! Really, totally awful!" The dam on her emotions finally burst. "'Else' brought Emma's yearbook from "St. Andrew's" and we picked out all the things we wanted to do next year. No, no; that was yesterday." Her voice wobbled. She hadn't meant to tell her mother anything. Bozz, now upset too, squirmed in her arms. Annie rubbed his warm head for a moment then put him down beside his food dish.

"Darling, I am truly sorry about all this. Come; sit down a minute. I'll pour us a cuppa."

Annie considered this an apology of sorts but held firm. She wouldn't let her mother off the hook yet. "So what school *will* I go to next year?"

"The local one; "St. Rule's"; it's the only choice." She brought two mugs of tea to the table.

"It'll be full of the fisherman's kids. I won't know a soul. And I bet they won't have a choir or…or a swimming pool. Oh, Mummy…" It was close to a wail.

"I'm so sorry, darling," she said again. Daddy and I hate upsetting you like this."

"And I hate the way you've spoiled everything!"

"Now, Annie, that's not fair, and you know it."

"I don't care. Nothing's fair now, is it?" said Annie pouting in earnest.

Annie's mother pulled a handkerchief out of her apron pocket and started blowing her nose. "You are quite right, dearest. Nothing is fair at all."

Annie had a strong feeling her mother wasn't talking about "St. Andrew's Academy" any more.

"I've just been speaking to Aunt Grace."

So she was right. There was something else.

Her mother took a long, slow sip of her tea. "She wondered how you would feel about having Moira here for a while."

"Moira?" What had this had to do with anything? "You mean now?"

Her mother nodded.

"Do you mean *just* Moira?"

"Just Moira."

Moira was Annie's only cousin. She was six, with long blonde pigtails and big blue eyes. Like Annie, she was an only child, and they both enjoyed being each other's cousin, despite the age gap. But now? Annie wasn't in any mood to be the caring older person; it was an effort just to ask about her.

"So why the hurry?"

"There has been an outbreak of polio in Kirkaren." Her mother dabbed at her nose again. "Several children are getting ill and the doctors are not holding out much hope that they will ever be well again."

Annie fidgeted. The conversation was getting too serious; it crowded in on her anger and making it difficult to answer properly. "We talked about polio at school this year but I never thought I'd know anyone who... " She swallowed then asked, "Moira hasn't got it, has she?"

"No she hasn't, but Aunt Grace is extremely worried. Polio is a highly contagious disease and infection spreads even more quickly in the cities."

Annie recalled Miss Sinclair talking about an illness called *infantile paralysis* that most often attacked young children. It started like flu but could go on to paralyze legs and arms and even lungs *within the first week,* her teacher had said. And there could be terrible pain too *and* the real possibility of death.

"I know." Annie was feeling worse by the moment. "It's horrible." Dreadful images were flashing through her mind as she thought back to the lesson. Images of patients whose lungs had collapsed, who had to be put into enormous machines that looked like tunnels, machines called iron lungs that forced their breath in and out to keep them alive. What if Moira...

"So parents are trying to get their children out to the country," her mother continued, drowning out Annie's recollections, "to the seaside or wherever they can get away from crowded conditions." She fingered her handkerchief. "Grace and Peter aren't in a position to leave their jobs at the hospital, especially now, so Moira will come without them."

Annie took a deep breath. "When will she be coming?"

"Next week, I expect. Peter has to arrange for the time off to drive Moira here. Grace can't even manage that. They are short staffed at the moment and every nurse is needed. But, honey, with all the rooms filled with guests I'll probably have to put her in with you." She paused. "That *will* be alright, won't it?"

Annie closed her eyes to avoid the pointed gaze.

Here they were again, pushing her to accept things. What about *her* summer holiday? She loved Moira but she was only six. What would they do all day?

"How long do you think she'll need to stay?"

"I really don't know. Until the danger has passed, I suppose. I can't be any more exact than that."

"That could be my whole summer, couldn't it?" Annie said her dismay growing.

"Yes, it could. Oh, sweetie," her mother's voice was strained, "you've had an awful lot to deal with, haven't you? If I could have made things different I would have but all I can think of now is how to help keep Moira safe."

"I know; it's just that…" that she felt a selfish beast for caring more about herself than her little cousin.

"Annie, I want to be able to tell Aunt Grace that you will make Moira welcome."

"Then tell her." Wow, that didn't come out well.

"I beg your pardon?" But just then the kitchen door clicked open and Molly breezed in.

"Good afternoon, Madam!" A tall, sturdily built woman, her dark hair in a neat bun, pulled a tartan scarf through her coat sleeve. "What shall I get to first? Set the dinner tables? Wash those dishes?"

"The tables, Molly; Aileen will do the dishes." Annie's mother was a study in self-control as she turned back to her daughter. "Honey, would you mind getting the napkins for…"

But Annie had already picked up her school bag and was gone.

* * *

Whenever Annie had issues to think about she would go to the beach. That was one thing she *did* love about her new home. It sat on a dead end street overlooking the sea. She had only to cross the street, run down the grassy brae to the seawall and jump onto the sand.

And there certainly were issues now with the news of Moira tumbling on top of all the "St. Andrew's" stuff; then flouncing out of the kitchen after answering her mother back. If Molly hadn't arrived when she did there might have been a nasty row.

Annie meandered down the grassy hill, hopped off the sea wall onto the beach and kicked off her sandals. She pushed her toes into the warm sand, feeling its gritty caress against her skin. All around her lay the beach and farther out the chain of rocks that protected it from the full rush of the breaking waves.

She stood, hands at her waist, and took in great gulps of the fresh salty air. She could feel the tightness in her chest unwind. She shaded her eyes from the sun and looked out to sea. Then from around the headland to the north a cluster of sailboats appeared. The wind caught in their sails making them skim along the water, overtaking or falling behind, criss-crossing one another as they raced. Some of the hulls were painted deep blue or scarlet while others just gleamed in woody gold. Their huge canvass sails stretched tight in the wind, then, as the boats tacked and turned around the marker buoys, the racket of their flapping was loud enough to carry all the way to shore.

Boats had always been part of her life because of her father. Before all this busy time to make ends meet, Sandy McLeod had turned his love for the sea into building model boats. Right now Annie would have loved one of those models, to hold and call her own. It would be wonderful to sail it and see it dancing with the wind like one of those racing yachts in the bay. Could she ask for such a gift? No; not one of her father's precious creations. They were *not toys* she had been told many times. They were to look at and admire, to hold perhaps but certainly not to play with.

Then the idea struck her. What about building a small boat herself; one that she and Moira could have fun with together? They needed *something* to do to fill in all those hours. As designer and builder she could show Moira how to sail it and if it was mostly *for* her young cousin maybe it wouldn't be such a babyish idea to play with it together? But would there be time to make even the simplest craft before Moira arrived?

Over the years Annie had done a lot of watching while her father created his models with all their tiny, perfect parts. She'd loved those special hours working with him, holding some of the intricate pieces, or searching through the labeled drawers for needed items if his hands were too busy to find them. He'd called her his "girl Friday". But that had all ended after the big move.

All the way back up the hill to the house Annie's mind worked on the problem her sadness easing off a bit with each fresh idea. She would find some wood scraps in her father's workshop and use some of his tools. Just a few. She'd keep it simple. Of course he may not want her working there on her own but in her present mood Annie didn't care much about that.

*   *   *

"How was the beach, sweetie?" Mrs. Macleod acknowledged her daughter for a fraction of a second before slipping into a starched apron for the dinner hour. "Aileen, did you remember to put out fresh napkins?"

"Yes, Madam."

"And where's Molly? I need her right this minute."

So there weren't going to be any consequences for her rudeness. That was a relief. "There was a boat race but not many people on the beach yet." Annie replied to the question now forgotten. She took a fork from the drawer and skewered a piece of baked fish from pan on the stove.

Her mother smiled, "Appetite back?"

"A bit, maybe."

"I'm heading out to class now, Margaret," her father's voice called from the doorway, "I'll be back around nine, give or take. Oh, Annie; didn't see you, so before I go," he was holding the door open now, "are you interested in coming to the Station with me tomorrow morning?"

Annie considered the offer. This was Daddy's way of saying how sorry he was about everything and she might have said yes, right off, if she hadn't had this new idea in mind.

He picked up his briefcase with his free hand. "I've got some repairs to do on *Largo*. I thought you might like to come and work on the boat with me?"

Annie hesitated again.

"Look I've got to go…think about it." He pecked her on the cheek then wheeled so the door slammed. Then came the crunch of gravel under car tires and he was gone.

Margaret McLeod turned to her daughter. "Daddy would like you to join him, you know," she said, smiling encouragement.

"I suppose." Annie licked her fishy fork then dropped it in the sink.

"Oh dear, I forgot to tell Sandy to stop by Gran's with that peat moss," said her mother, her attention diverted from Annie again. Then without missing a beat she added, "Annie darling, be a dear and go and ring the gong for dinner. The guests will be thinking we're not feeding them tonight."

Annie meandered into the front hall and picked up the suede mallet in front of the huge brass gong. She struck its dimpled face four or five times and listened to the mellow sound reverberate through the house. Doors opened, lounge chairs scraped back and the 'unwelcome' guests drifted in to dinner.

With the echoes of the gong still in her head Annie left the house and went out to the garden swing to read in the lingering summer light. She'd brought the copy of Prince Caspian she'd found on her school desk that afternoon; a hundred hours ago, it seemed. A piece of paper, torn from a notebook, fell from one of the pages. *Dear Annie,* it read, *if you can't talk to me at least write and tell me what's wrong. Please. Your forever friend, Else.* Annie burst into tears.

Chapter Five

Permission Not Granted

Over breakfast Annie declined her father's offer to help him work on the rescue boat. It would be the perfect time to get started in his workshop undetected. She was beginning to feel enthusiastic about the project, imagining the final results and Moira's admiration. And the fact that her dad might not like her messing around with his stuff added a thrill of guilty excitement.

* * *

The workshop door squeaked on its hinges when Annie pushed it open. The room was dark, the dusty curtains that covered the two small windows blocking most of the light from outside. She flung them open. A patch of sunshine splashed onto a set of shelves on the far wall covered with the most amazing collection of model boats.

* * *

Annie thought back to the day when she and her father had brought in the boxes of models and set each boat carefully on the shelves. Together they had un-crated his cabinet with the tiny drawers that held his modeling tools and the endless parts that were needed for building. They had pushed it against the wall under the shelves, next to a bench of sorts and a box of wood scraps left by the previous owner. The other boxes they just piled into corners.

"So that's it, honey," her father sighed. "It's all here but I doubt I'll have much time to enjoy it anymore." He closed the door and he and Annie walked back to the big house. That was two years ago.

*   *   *

Annie reached up and pulled on the cord con-nected to a bulb overhead. Light flooded into the abandoned room. She looked around taking in the stacks of boxes, the dusty shelves and models and an even dustier corduroy chair. A twinge of guilt rip-pled though her. She shouldn't be here; not without her Dad.

But, no, she had a plan and she was going to get on with it.

She had been right about box of wood scraps. It was still under the bench. The previous owner obviously hadn't been a fine carpenter or an expert model builder, the rusted vice screwed to the workbench being proof, but then neither was Annie. She picked through the box hunting for a pieces of wood. She needed one that could form a basic floating platform, then another that might be attached to fill out the hull and finally one that might be slotted through or glued below, somehow, as a keel. She wished she had paid closer attention to her father because already she wondered if she had bitten off a whole lot more than she could chew.

Where to begin? She delayed by looking for tools next; a small hammer and saw from her father's cabinet along with a chisel, a few nails and some glue.

It would have to be a very basic boat; nothing fancy, though she *could* study some of the models on the shelf overhead if she needed help.

Annie placed her supplies on the workbench and found a stool to sit on that raised her to a good working height. The wood pieces lay before her. She puzzled over how to start.

Basic design, she repeated; biggest piece on the bottom. She placed it firmly on the work surface. It seemed a shade long, but perhaps that would give it a streamlined appearance. The good thing was the sides were nice and straight with a pointed bit already at one end.

In her mind Annie replayed the picture of the sleek racing yachts she had watched the day before. From a distance their lines and shapes had looked simple enough to copy. Up close it was more tricky. Still, there was always sandpaper and a good coat of paint if her work looked rough at the edges.

Her attention had not been on the hammer. The steel head missed the nail and came down painfully on her thumb. Gripping the handle more firmly she watched its descent with experienced caution and sent the nail right through the wood fixing the 'stage one' boat snuggly to the top of the bench!

In frustration she pried the 'boat' off with the claw of the hammer. She hadn't expected it to be so awkward. When it came up the tip of the nail still showed. Rats.

Annie struggled to dig it out from the top deck but it was too small to grip. She turned the pieces of wood over and knocked it in further then held her work up to the light. *Now* the top piece didn't line up with the one below! It would throw the boat off balance for crumbs' sake! How could sticking a few pieces of wood together give her so much grief!

*   *   *

An hour passed, then nearly two. She gazed in dismay at her crude vessel. It was *nothing* like the way she'd pictured it! And as soon as she set it in the water it would probably flip over too. Even at six, Moira would definitely not be impressed.

Much out of sorts she thumped down on the dusty corduroy chair in the corner.

"Yeow," came the protest from Bozz.

"Yeow right back, Bozz. You scared me to bits slinking in here without letting me know." Annie checked the door but it was still closed. "So tell me, cat, just how did you get in here?"

"Yeow?"

Looking further she noticed a loose board along the adjoining wall that had been pried back. The opening was just cat-size. "Ah, I see. So this is your usual hangout, then?" she said, stroking his soft fur.

But he was not interested in the conversation or in sharing his chair space. Bozz dropped to the floor, then, in a single leap landed on one of the shelves alongside the models.

"Take care you crazy animal," Annie's voice was soft with affection, "if you knock anything over I won't take the blame for you." But it was clear Bozz did this often. Not one whisker grazed the boats as he padded along the shelf to his chosen resting spot his black tail like a periscope above him.

How she loved that animal, scrappy and independent as he could be at times. She would never forget that day last spring when Bozz came into her life. Annie had been on another of her beach wanders. She had heard the pitiful cries and had followed the sound until she reached a nest of seaweed where three tiny kittens lay huddled into one another. Two of them were quite still but the third, eyes still closed, reached out with its tiny paws and kneaded at the weedy mat. Its body crawled over the others drawing the last morsel of heat from their inert shapes then it tumbled mewling onto the sand.

"You poor, wee might!" Annie cried, her eyes prickling. She reached over and picked up the almost weightless bundle. It barely filled her outstretched hands. She drew it to her chest while it fought her, its tiny claws scratching and its legs pushing against her.

"Where is your mother to leave you so?" crooned Annie.

But if there had been one nearby she was nowhere in sight. Annie set her small bundle down then began scraping a hole into the sand. Tears welled up in her eyes and down her cheeks. Her sadness hurt. She had no idea if it would be better to bury the two kittens or let them wash away in the next tide but something made her dig anyway.

Finished, she set a heavy stone over the burial spot and reached again for the feisty kitten and took it home; her Bozz, her little survivor.

*   *   *

Annie squooshed further down into the tattered corduroy chair. Boat building just wasn't one of her skills.

"I better clear up this mess, huh?" she grumbled to the recumbent Bozz. There was no point getting in trouble when she'd got nothing to show for it. Annie was about to drop the pieces she had been working on back into the box when she had second thoughts. If her father came out here, unlikely but possible, he might see her clumsy attempt if it were lying on top so she'd best tip everything out first and bury it underneath. It was a big box, packed with stuff. When she up-ended it piles of odds and ends tumbled out over the floor, dust flew and a startled Bozz leapt out of his sleeping spot.

"Bozz! Look out or you'll…"

The model seemed to hang suspended in the air for a split second. Annie lunged for it and missed. They both crashed to the floor. She whacked her knees and cried out in pain. Bozz shot out his 'cat door'.

"Oh Bozz," Annie groaned pulling herself up. She stared in horror at the model lying beside her, its mast broken, its rails bent and with a gash along one side of the hull.

"Oh Bozz, Daddy is going to *kill* me!" She rubbed her knees, a lump building in her throat, sick with worry and hurt all together. The dust that still hung in the air made her sneeze. "Whad ab I goig to *do*?" She held her stuffed head in her hands and gulped back sobs.

When she opened her eyes again a powdery film had settled on the model. She picked it up and blew the dust away from around its decks and damaged rigging. The sunlight caught the specks and made them shimmer, like stars all around.

"Oh!" She turned the boat in her hands, "You're the *William Morr*, aren't you?" she said reading the name on the stern plate. "I'm afraid I have wrecked you for certain. And now Daddy is going to wreck me when he sees what I've done; *if* he sees what I've done."

*   *   *

"You're very quiet, dear" Annie's mother remarked during a shared, late supper.

"Sorry, just thinking."

"What about?" her dad said smiling.

Annie froze. She could feel his eyes looking right through her into the workshop and around to the back of the shelf where she had hidden the *William Morr*. "I'm working on something for Moira. It's complicated. And it's a secret," she added forcing a grin.

"Can't wait to see it then, kiddo." Her father winked at her across the table.

*   *   *

Annie's supper was settling heavily in her stomach but she continued to eat so that her mother wouldn't fuss. As soon as possible she excused herself from the table and returned to the *scene of the crime*. The work-room door creaked ominously as she entered.

The seed of a new idea was growing in her mind. Maybe she could solve two problems at the same time. Some sort of a repair seemed the only decent thing to do and, if this worked, *maybe* it would be alright to share the boat with Moira? After all that had been the purpose of this whole project, hadn't it? Would her father even remember this particular model? It must have been sitting up there for ages gathering dust.

Annie carried the sad little vessel out into the setting sunshine. With a soft rag she pushed gently between the mast and the sculpted details on the deck. She blew more dust away then let her fingers stroke the gleaming hull. If she squinted she could see little pieces of herself in the shiny sides.

"Well, *Bill*, what do you think?" Annie liked this friendlier version of the name. Maybe, with luck and a bit of effort, she could make it seaworthy again. Annie's hopes were on the rise. After all, rescue was her specialty, wasn't it? She supported the battered wooden boat in her hands, examining it from all angles. She would start by taking away the broken pieces of mast and torn sail; 'clear the decks' for action as her father liked to say.

Anticipation tingled through her.

Bozz trotted across the lawn and rubbed against Annie's legs.

*   *   *

Annie soon realized that her 'rescue' operation would not be easy. And there would be no point rushing things either and making her repairs look sloppy. Moira might not say anything, but her father certainly would.

But she was going to need help. Seeing a model being built was not at all like making one yourself; she'd found that out in spades. So, could she even *mend* this one? Could there be some books *somewhere* in this darn workshop she could turn to?

"Hey books!" Annie started pulling boxes out from under the shelves. She flipped open their cardboard lids searching. It took a while.

"Finally!" she yanked a dusty carton out into the middle of the room. Under the pull string light she sat on the floor and emptied out paperbacks, hard covered books, even coffee table sized volumes one after the other. There were sea stories, books showing the parts of a sailboat and boats of all kinds and thankfully, several on model building. One or two of these suggested materials to use, tools needed and procedures to follow if you were starting from scratch. It was like Christmas.

*   *   *

Back in the workshop, next morning, Annie laid out the *William Morr* on the worktable to figure out how best to remove the damaged pieces. She opened one or two drawers looking for the tiny tools she'd just read about; the ones she used to hand to her father. She would need something small but very sharp to dig out the broken mainmast and some tiny pliers to straighten the bent stanchions. Then the sails would have to be removed and reattached to the new mast. Wow, this was going to be a job and a half!

By the next day the removal was pretty well complete and Annie had gone on to the gash in the hull. Her hands shook at times from excitement or nerves, she wasn't sure which. It was such finicky work. So different from the way she had started out all slap dash and full of confidence.

She fixed the keel carefully into the old vice to hold the model steady and stroked ever so gently with the finest sandpaper till the hull felt smooth again. To restore the colour she'd found some tiny pots of stain and an incredibly small brush. She got a crick in her neck from holding steady and using teeny weenie strokes.

*   *   *

The stain had dried by next morning. She held her handiwork to the light. It was still minus the mast and sails, but she'd take things one step at a time. And right now she had one pretty amazing sailing hull to take out on its first sea trial.

She looked around the workshop: work table tidy; drawers pushed back in; nothing left on the floor; tools cleaned and returned.

Closing the door with her free hand, beach bag with boat wrapped inside in the other, Annie crossed the garden and nearly bumped smack into Aileen hanging sheets on the clothes line.

"Off to the beach are you, then?"

Annie gulped. "Y-Yes… I…I brought a towel in case I go swimming," she held the bag up.

"Aren't you the brave one. The water is that chill, lassie, ye'll no have much company."

"I don't mind." Annie backed away then took off at a run across the lawn and on past the house to the grassy hill leading to the beach. The gulls screamed overhead in a deep blue sky and the waves hissed onto the shore.

Chapter Six

First Sea Trial

Annie judged the best place for the 'maiden voyage' would be at the far north end of the beach where a particular group of large rocks curved inward from the sea. When the tide was in it made a wide, deep bathing area but now the water was shallow enough to expose a low sand bar and allow her to walk out to the rocks and tide pools. High on top of the reef she hoped to find a small protected piece of ocean. She kicked off her sandals and splashed into the chilly water. The sand scraped under her feet. She wandered about enjoying the sensation, following the scratchy patches wherever they led.

When she reached the rocks they towered over her. The climb would be tricky with a boat in tow. She pulled the canvass handles of the bag over her head and pushed the load against her back to free her hands to climb. She reached for the first hand hold and pulled up her toes searching for a ledge to anchor her. Then another reach and another; hands pulling up, toes locked on. Progress was slow but once she stepped out on top the view was stunning. The ocean crashed against the sloping face on the sea side filling the rock pools. Looking back to the beach where she'd come from and the sudden drop she'd scaled took her breath away.

She started across the slippery kelp covered boulders, their air-filled bladders popping under her bare feet. Strands of bright green mermaid's hair draped over tide pool edges and waved in the water below. It took some searching but eventually she found a pool the right depth, lined with sand and with rocks around it flat enough to move around easily.

Annie pulled the precious bundle from the beach bag. "Well, *Bill*, get ready to feel the sea beneath you for a change." She kneeled down and set him gently on the surface. He swayed a little but didn't tip.

"So, how's that chum? Bet the water feels nicer than that dusty old shelf."

Since this part of the beach was still deserted there was no one to notice a gangly twelve year old leaning over a rock pool talking to a boat! But very soon it would be crowded with swimmers and sunbathers and the doors to the now empty beach huts would be draped with colourful towels drying in the sunshine.

She put her hand against the stern, straightened the rudder, and pushed gently. *Bill* skimmed toward the other side of the pool.

"Straight as an arrow… Bravo!"

Annie walked around, leaned over and pushed a bit harder sending her boat back to the start line. It sailed the whole distance just brushing the rock on the far side. But could it manage a turn? Annie adjusted the rudder hinge and nudged the stern. It moved off slowly in a wide arc and sailed parallel to the curved edges of the pool the whole way. Annie was thrilled to bits. *Bill* moved, as though steered from within, without tipping, or banging into rocks, or stopping before he should.

*   *   *

But the tide was busily at work too. While Annie was discovering the perfect balance between hull, keel and rudder, the sea had crept back around the rocks and in over the sandbar.

When the first wave broke and showered them with salty spray, Annie screamed. Then another surged up over the rocks. This one crashed into their pool filling it till its edges disappeared. The rocks were awash with the sea. *Bill* was rocking a lot. He was not ready for the advanced course yet.

"Hang on!" Annie leaned into the frothy water. The waves gushed across the pools now, spilling down the rock face onto the sand as they curled round from the ocean.

It was the third wave that picked up the boat. It pushed it ahead in its wake clear over the rock wall that Annie had scaled and down into the sea swirling below.

Annie scrambled to the edge of the drop and looked down. The water was too deep for wading now. It had all happened so fast; the turning tide; being swamped; *Bill* being swept away.

It was hard to see the small boat as it tumbled about in the water. At any moment it could be sucked out by the retreating waves, over the sandbar and out to sea; gone. No proud *William Morr*; no dazzling sailing vessel for Moira to play with.

How totally stupid of her not to have thought ahead! Of course the rocks would disguise the incoming tide. She'd watched this happening from the beach hundreds of times.

It was all too clear now that to save the boat she would have to dive down into the tossing sea below. Trouble was she'd never actually done it from this place before. Were there rocks scattered across the sand? How deep was it? Should she risk a dive or just jump? In either event was the unpleasant thought that the sodden weight of her clothes would hold her down and slow her strokes.

And her body knew she was in trouble too. Her knees started to tremble and with every moment of delay the shaking grew worse and her worry increased. The incoming tide could easily pull her out to sea or crush her against the sharp rocks when it drew back. Struggling to control a mounting fear she removed her shorts and blouse and stepped closer to the edge.

For one last second she felt the rock support her bare feet then she jumped out into space. Air whistled round her followed by the hard smack of water. It closed over her, the cold, salty gush making her head pound and her eyes sting.

She fought back panic; the unfamiliar feeling she was about to drown. Her confidence washed away with every labored stroke against the tumbling water. She fought for breath and heaved her head upward against the force of the waves.

When she broke the surface her eyes opened and her legs kicked out the automatic rhythms they knew. But still the tide sucked beneath. She shut her mouth hard to keep the sea out and searched ahead for the outline of *Bill* moving toward the beach. And suddenly, there he was! He was skimming forward, surfing with the in-going waves! It looked as if this was just how he intended to wind up his maiden voyage.

Then the waves pulled back and *Bill* stalled.

Her fingertips stretched to touch the boat and keep it ahead against the tide that tugged at both of them. It no sooner moved them forward than it dragged them back again toward the now submerged rocks and the outer bay.

Annie had never worked so hard to move; never been so at war with the water. She took a stroke then reached to push; then another stroke and another push. In agonizing slow motion the beach inched closer toward them.

When Annie finally felt the beach press up against her chest her arms still reached forward. She lay for a few moments her breath rasping painfully in her throat then pulled herself up onto the sundried sand letting the warmth soothe her.

But the incoming tide had a few more tricks up its sleeve. It swam round Annie's legs and began to cover the *William Morr* in the wash of retreating sand and sodden cloth. Alert, she grabbed for the boat, tightening her hand round the gritty wooden hull and pulled it toward her. "You can't have him!" she shouted to the frothing sea, "He's Moira's... and he's mine!"

*   *   *

With immense relief Annie shook out the gift of a pair of shorts the tide had returned to her. She picked off the scraps of seaweed, shook out sand and seawater and struggled back into them. She shivered in her undershirt and wished the tide had been more generous.

As Annie slowly got to her feet, steadying herself to let her head clear, it struck her she might be in for trouble at home. It had been ages since she'd left the house. No doubt her mother was busy serving lunch for the summer guests and wondering why Annie hadn't appeared for hers. Then there were the chores she'd left undone.

"But it was worth it, wasn't it?" Annie said grinning down at *Bill* as she plowed through the mounded sand and across the sea weedy blankets intertwined with gull feathers and bits of tar. Her soggy, salty clothes scraped at her skin and leaked wetness down her legs. A door from one of the beach huts slammed in a gust of wind and made her jump. Her hair dripped and she shivered despite the sunshine.

When they arrived at the steps leading up from the beach she stopped to put on her sandals. What sandals? She wasn't carrying any. Annie groaned. The sea had stolen those too.

Annie squeezed water from her clothes and swung her head about to spray it out of her cropped hair. She climbed the hill and the grey stone walls of *Lin Cove* appeared over the brae wall its huge double front doors wide open in welcome; for the guests, of course. Annie was expected to use the side door to the kitchen. But not this time. The lounge was empty during lunch. She would take the shortcut to the stairs and her room and if she left a few sandy footprints on the carpet, too bad.

*   *   *

Annie dashed up to her bedroom for a blouse, hid *Bill* in her closet then made her way to the kitchen hoping to blend in with the mealtime hubbub. And no one paid Annie any attention at all. Not even Aileen who noticed everything. There was a faraway look in the woman's eyes as she whistled *"Don't Fence Me In"* for the hundredth time, to a sink brimming with pots and pans.

The tantalizing aroma of shepherd's pie hung in the air. Annie's mouth watered. Molly swung in through the dining room door balancing a heavy tray of dirty dishes. The main course was over.

Annie hung back, considering her options. No sign of any shepherd's pie. Her tummy rumbled. So it was too late for the main course but over on the far counter, spread out and cooling on wire racks were the teacakes her mother had baked using those extra rations. They were Annie's absolute favorite: the melt-in-your-mouth pastry with raspberry jam and almond sponge collapsed all Annie's caution. Living in a hotel had *some* benefits.

"Dinna' even think about it, lassie," Aileen said interrupting her serenade just long enough to save the cakes.

Annie dropped her hovering hand and turned from the counter.

"...*gaze at the moon till I lose my senses...*" Aileen continued with the syncopated pot clatter as backup.

But on such a day of daring Annie felt bold enough to chance it. She felt a rush of excitement, a sort of bubble and fizz inside her. She glanced back at Aileen entertaining herself with her concert in the suds, then, with unaccustomed nerve Annie grabbed two warm tarts and dashed out into the garden.

Bozz was curled up under the bird feeder.

Barefoot Annie plunked herself down on the damp grass beside her cat, removed a tart from her pocket and took her first bite of contraband.

"Annie! And just *where* have you been all morning?" her mother called to her from the direction of the rose garden.

Too late to hide what remained of the tart Annie stuffed it in her mouth and dropped her head. Her mother stood right above her, frowning, with a jug of roses for the dinner tables in one hand and shears in the other. It made a prickly combination.

Bozz, however, was enchanted. One of the branches had slipped from its nest and dangled just above paw height. Bozz sprung. Rose thorns, wet blossoms, leaves and stems in higgledy-piggledy fashion tumbled all over the lawn.

"Bozz, I swear you are the most exasperating cat in Christendom," Mrs. McLeod stormed, gathering up the muddle of roses in her apron and marching toward the house.

Free from the scolding she supposed was her due

Annie extracted the second, now badly crumbled tart and bit into it. It didn't disappoint. She rolled onto her back on the grass and scratched Bozz under his chin.

Bozz purred. His black silky fur oozed heat. Annie rested her face against the animal's side and let the purring rumble relax her. She thought she might like to be a cat in another life, able to wander off in the moonlight and experience the night without anyone questioning her reasons or fretting for her safety. Maybe she could leap up on walls with ease instead of suffering the scraped knees and fingers that plagued her present efforts? Yes, definitely a cat.

Bozz stretched out to double his length and sighed. Annie curled up, catlike, beside him and closed her eyes.

Chapter Seven

Hamish

Next day it poured. Annie looked out from her bedroom window at the glistening street. Normally she hated "indoor days" but now, with critical repairs to get on with, it didn't matter at all. She retrieved *Bill* from her bedroom cupboard and wrapping her raincoat around them both slipped back out to the workshop. All clear this time. No sheets; no Aileen.

The hardest part was going to be re-attaching the mast. She dabbed glue into the hole she had cleaned out and began gently pushing the mast back in place. The glue would have to dry thoroughly before the next step. She would deal with the stays to support it later. She propped the boat behind a pile of boxes and returned to her room.

Annie picked up the next sailing book from the pile she had brought back from the workshop. This one was about technique and all the sorts of things you'd need to do while actually handling a boat alone. She was glad of the diagrams and used her new knowledge of which parts were which. There were so many new words beyond bow, stern, sails and hulls. Sheets were lines not bedclothes she learned; and lines weren't words in a row but ropes to secure a boat to a dock or adjust its sails.

She sat on the window seat. Between chapters she watched the rain beat against the panes of glass. These small windows felt safer than the ones in her main floor bedroom. In the winter, when gales howled in off the sea, those wide panes would bend and the wind would whistle through the sashes. The glass had never actually broken but her parents insisted the curtains be drawn just in case.

"The walls are twenty-seven inches thick," her father told her, "but there's just a single pane of glass between you and the wind."

She shivered. "How old *is* this house?"

"A hundred years at least," he said, "…or older. The town has been here for hundreds. It was the shire seat, you know."

Annie didn't. Next to sailboats and model building her father's great love was history and he would launch into lengthy explanations if she let him. She learned on that occasion that the town had been granted its Royal Charter by Robert the Bruce in 1310!

* * *

There was a knock at her door and her mother poked her head in. "You're not spending all day up here reading are you?"

"Sorry; lost track of time. I'll be right down."

She had avoided her chores completely the day before spending a disgracefully idle afternoon in the garden snoozing and recovering with Bozz. No wonder her mother was after her now.

But Annie didn't resent it as much as she used to. The "Moira Project" had triggered a real change. The anger toward her parents was fading and in its place was a growing self confidence. She could "do" things; like leap into uncharted waters and swim against a rising tide! And, after reading the latest book from her father's workshop, she might even follow in the author's footsteps one day and attempt a solo crossing of the North Sea.

This 'new' Annie was eager to show her parents her generous side. She found Aileen hoovering the red plush carpet in the lounge, muttering about all the sand. Feeling a bit guilty Annie offered to take over the noisy machine.

"It's no' that reliable, Annie. I best get on wi' it mysel'."

"Then I'll collect the dirty sheets if you like," and she set off at the run to strip the linen off the beds and take up fresh sheets. She polished silver in the dining room and rubbed her arms sore making the brass tray-table in the lounge gleam. As she worked it was hard to keep her eyes off the shiny wooden cabinet with the radio gramophone under the bay window. Listening to her favorite program on "Children's Hour" was another pleasure now out of bounds for the summer!

And to prove her goodwill beyond doubt Annie

offered to do the dreaded 'potato job'. Her father had bought a "sort of automatic" potato-peeling machine but it only sanded off the easy bits leaving the eyes and bruised parts to be done by hand. Annie leaned into the machine, with its fousty, earthy smell and pulled out a few grubby spuds. It was going to be a long day.

*   *   *

By the next morning the clouds had moved off. With her fine record of chores behind her Annie went down to check that the glue on the mast was dry. She wanted to try *Bill* out again, somewhere safer this time, before moving on to further repairs. She used a box for protection, having lost the bag along with her sandals *and blouse* last time, and set off for the beach.

But halfway down the footpath there came the squeal of bicycle brakes and the thump of metal on grass.

"Hey, Annie McLeod," called a boy with tousled red hair, grinning all over his freckled face.

"Hamish Findlay!"

"Got your hair chopped I see," he said.

"Grrr! Mother's bright idea. So when did you arrive?" She could have sworn he was still wearing last summer's scruffy brown shorts and the same faded Brit Air cap his dad gave him years ago. "I thought your parents might've rented out your house."

"Na, changed their minds. Dad's back with the airline again; same Trans-Atlantic flights. We'll be here a while, I think."

The Findlays were world travelers. As a result

Hamish spent extra long periods at boarding school, even over holidays at times, so that when he did come home friends were in short supply.

They'd known each other from way back because their fathers served together in the Royal Navy; Sandy McLeod as Executive Officer on board *H.M.S. Dunvale* and Commander David Findlay, in the Fleet Air Arm. Those dangerous times could make friendships intense, so, even though the Findlays' life style was quite different from the McLeods', the families still spent time together. And now Hamish would be around again. Her summer was getting busier.

"That's terrific! We'll do stuff together," blurted Annie before thinking.

"So; where've you been? I looked in all the usual places."

Annie hesitated. She wanted to keep the boat business to herself. "On the beach, fooling around, collecting stuff; you know."

"What'ya got there?" Hamish looked at the box Annie held.

"Oh, nothing much. You wouldn't be interested."

"I would so. Let's see," he reached for the box.

Annie set it down on the path and reluctantly peeled back the newspapers that held *Bill* in place.

"Hey; neat. Looks kinda unfinished though. Where'd you get it?"

"Oh, it's an old one of Dad's. It was broken. I'm fixing it, sort of."

"What for?"

Explaining wasn't something Annie felt like doing. "Oh, I dunno. Something to do I guess."

"Really? So can we try it?"

She should have known her 'project' would be right up Hamish' alley. "We-ell, I wasn't going to the beach. I..." she trailed off knowing this sounded dumb.

"So why bring the boat?"

Annie shuffled her feet.

"Aw c'mon, Annie. Who're you kidding? Here, let me!" And with that Hamish grabbed the open box clean out of Annie's grasp and was back on his bike in a flash. Riding one-handed, with the box in the other, he spun off down the hill.

"Stop you idiot! You'll drop it!" shouted Annie, running at full tilt behind him.

*   *   *

And Hamish chose the sailing place too. He was impossible. It was at the far south end of the beach and surrounded by huge rocks that hid it from view until you were almost right there. Occasionally some of the older boys from the village hung around skipping stones or getting into shoving matches near the water's edge. It was a not a pool either but a wide dark pond, an expanse of water, that opened to the sea on the far side. How ghastly if her boat got marooned in the middle or drifted out to sea! Every ounce of her prayed this wouldn't happen.

Hamish had already pulled the model from the box and was holding it over the water's edge when Annie caught up. "Hang on Hamish! You can't just plunk it in."

He moved back then sat on the rocks holding the boat to his chest. "You don't trust me?" he grinned.

"No I don't. And besides it's mine so I should go first."

She took the boat and leaned over the water. There was no sand at the bottom. It was deep and murky and probably hid creepy things that bit.

"Come on, Annie, whatya' waiting for?" Hamish said poking at the seaweedy mat he was sitting on.

"Just a sec, *okay.*"

Then a crab scuttled over Hamish's leg and he leapt up, "Yah! Move off!" he shouted and ran kicking after it.

Annie had to be certain *Bill* would make it clear to the far rocky edge. "Ready?" she whispered, her cheek brushing the tip of the mast. She straightened the rudder, gave him a hard push then crossed her fingers. And what a relief; there could have been some engine inside him by the way he moved off in a steady line seeming to gain speed as he went.

She plunked back down on the rocks, more relaxed, allowing herself to smile.

Hamish was back again, focused and intent on the boat's movements. "Wow, it really does move. You fixed this yourself Annie?"

"Yeah. It was a bit tricky, though. I'm not much with tools."

"You did a great job. Lucky your Dad lets you use his stuff."

She let that remark pass and kept her eyes fixed on *Bill*. It had seemed like a good idea to push him all the way across. Now she wasn't so sure. He was moving away awfully fast.

"Oh, Hamish…"

"What's up?"

"How are we going to get it back?"

"I can hike around, I think. But you should've thought of that before you pushed it so far," he accused.

"The rocks look slippery and the tide could be coming in," Annie cautioned.

"No problem. I'll take this stick. Or I could jump, maybe." Hamish yanked off his sandals.

"Stay with the rocks, Hamish."

"Na, this'll be faster. I'll swim over the deep bits. Oh, here, hang onto this, would ya?"

He tossed his cap at her then stepped into the water, shirt, shorts and all.

"It's not that easy in your clothes," Annie cautioned again.

A gust of wind caught the boat.

"I should've put a sail on somehow. It'd be easier to see." Annie shielded her eyes and squinted into the distance.

Hamish was taking giant, wobbly strides, through water that was thigh deep already.

"You okay?"

"Fine," but he sounded winded. Suddenly he splashed down into the water his arms flailing. "Yikes, that was a deep bit!"

"Watch out for your toes!"

"Wha'd'ya mean? I meant to do that!" Hamish never admitted he was wrong if he could help it. "Now, into the jaws of danger goes the intrepid Sir Hamish!"

"You're an idiot, *Sir Hamish*!"

Showers of seawater sprayed all around him as he floundered and tipped until he finally melted into a smooth crawl and was off.

Annie sighed. *He'd* certainly got the breathing right.

Hamish was a good way across when he caught up to it.

"Hey, AAAA...NNIE! I got it!" he yelled holding the boat over his head.

She cupped her hands, "Put him back in and push like mad!"

Bill was bearing down, fast, in her direction after the shove. There was even a small wake off his stern. At the last moment he turned in a half circle, his speed cut abruptly and came to a halt by her feet. Had the wind done that?

"Fantastic! Just wait till I get your sails back on!" she said lifting *Bill* out, water streaming down his shiny sides. Successful sea trial part two.

Hamish came in second, dripping all over the rocks. "Some rescue, huh?" He grabbed his cap and squashed it back on.

*   *   *

"Your boat have a name?" Hamish asked on their way back up the brae.

"*Bill*," Annie said before she meant to.

"*Bill*? Not much of a name for a boat like this?"

"His full name is '*William Morr*'. Look at the stern plate. I just shortened it. It's easier to say." For Moira she thought and hoped Hamish would stop asking questions.

"Oh, I see it. You're planning to fix him up some more, though?" he paused. "I could help, you know."

Work on her precious model with Hamish? Uh,

uh. "I'll think about it," Annie said. "You were super back there, by the way. That water looked too creepy for me."

"Yeah, it worked out." Hamish went on," So why don't we try sailing the *'William Morr'* there again? In a couple of days, say?"

They were at the top of the hill now. "Yeah, maybe. Look, I've gotta get going. Mum's forgotten about…"

"About what?" Hamish began, but Annie had already taken off. She was fast in her bare feet.

Chapter 8

A Risk

Annie caught the first faint skirls of the bagpipes in the air next morning and let the gooseberry pail drop. She'd finish the picking later. When the pipe band calls you have to follow.

She grabbed her bike, skidded over the gravel road outside the back gate and took off up the street towards town. The pipes grew louder. She was on the right track.

Her legs pumped furiously up "Conker Hill" under the chestnut trees that spilled their glossy brown seeds on the roadway every autumn. She crested onto High Street and on past Old St. Mary's churchyard, whizzed by Calder's Bakery, the fishmonger and the red pillar box before scraping to a stop in front of the ancient Town Hall at the crossroads. Up that road to the north lay "St. Andrews Academy", Annie thought for one painful moment before being drawn back to the joyous din.

The square echoed with *Tunes of Glory* and flashed with colour. The Drum Major led, his silver mace towering above his head; the kilt swinging tartan pipers followed.

Annie abandoned her bicycle behind the worn stone walls of the Town Hall. She skip hop stepped, the way they did in their country dance class, along the pavement as close to the heavenly racket as she dared without getting in their way. She was level with the drummers now. The booming rhythms gave her goose bumps.

There was old Jock Currie, the postman, with his elbow pressed into the bag of his pipes, his mouth blowing in that weird, out of time way with the music he was making. And that looked like Henry Morrison, from dance class, in the drum brigade. Annie was sure he was barely twelve. Lucky duck. And Mr. Gibson's shop assistant, she forgot his name, and the Aitken twins. My, but they all looked fine in their kilts; hardly the same people at all!

Now, where would they go next? Not in the direction of the harbour, certainly. The cobbled road was far too steep and the reek from lobster creels and fishing nets would take all their puff away. Annie imagined the drummers losing their footing, their instruments rolling headlong over the harbour walls in amongst the fishing boats with thunderous crashes.

To her delight they turned back along High Street. Annie ran with the crowd of village children along the streets that led right onto Lin Cove Crescent and past her very own house!

Nothing could compare with the skirl of the pipes

in Annie's opinion. She sat on the steps across from her house being part of it all. The entire band was moving in a winding path along the cliff above the sands. The strains of *The Dark Island* sounded wilder and sadder than ever mixing with the wind and surf. Then, abruptly the mace dropped and there was silence. The pipers and drummers turned and began marching away to the north, the loosened pipes swaying and the drum sticks clicking next to their tartan sides.

*   *   *

The excitement over, Annie ran back into town to collect her bicycle then delivered the mostly full pail of gooseberries to the kitchen. It was time to get back to the workshop. Moira would be arriving soon and she was nowhere near finished the repairs.

As usual Annie yanked on the pull-string bulb overhead to brighten the patchy sunlight that penetrated from outdoors. She was concerned about making changes to the boat and doubted her skills were up to the next level of improvements. *Bill* had moved so well in the water. What if she upset his balance when she put back the missing parts? But then you could hardly have a sailboat without sails, now, could you?

On the positive side her chances at keeping her work secret were good. The house was overflowing with early season hikers and this particular morning her dad was off fishing for mackerel with Tam, Molly's husband. Not that he'd come out here but it made her feel safer knowing he'd be gone several hours anyway.

Annie stared at her father's models carefully. She

lifted a couple down from the shelf to see exactly how they went together. She fingered the delicate masts and the rigging. They were all so perfect. "How does he *do* that?" Annie sighed. "How does it all come out so right?" Annie looked again at the pieces she'd removed. The storage drawers above the work table should have replacements.

Feeling like a thief again Annie pulled a few open. So many tiny pieces! As she picked up each one her mind hopped back and forth to the books she'd been reading; mainsails, staysails, sheets; how to attach the sails. Those, most fortunately, had survived the tumble from the shelf. She studied the pages open before her and crossed her fingers then she took whatever looked right and hoped for the best.

A whole day passed in concentrated effort. Bozz had claimed the brown chair again that afternoon and Annie glanced at him occasionally hoping he'd stay put and off the shelves. The models stood watch from their perches, a puff of wind from the open door disturbing the sails of one, a stray sunbeam glinting off the deck of another.

When she finished Annie was very pleased with herself. "You're a sailboat again, *Bill,*" she whispered running her fingers over all the new pieces of him, "my beautiful rescued sailboat!" She cleared a space at the back of the workbench, propped the *William Morr* against it and stood back to admire her handiwork. He looked amazing with mast, the boom and the rigging all in place and, perhaps, not *so* very different from the original?

*   *   *

The following day Annie fit in sea trial number three. To her relief all the added parts stayed attached and *Bill* sailed more perfectly than ever. This was one of the most fantastic things she had done in a long time. Moira would be thrilled and with luck maybe her father would come on side too.

Annie was relaxing on the canopied swing in the west garden, still basking in the glow of her success, when Hamish arrived unannounced. The *William Morr* lay in his box on the grass beside her.

"You've done some more fixing up," he said lifting the boat onto his lap and examining it.

"Mm-hm."

"Your Dad help you? It looks really professional," he whistled in admiration.

Annie was too happy with the results to be offended by Hamish's remarks. Besides she could hardly blame him for his question. Her Dad had been well known in the towns nearby for his remarkable model boats.

"No, but I did use some of his tools and some spare parts I found. You won't tell will you? Please? Daddy's very fussy about them and, truth is, I hadn't asked permission," Annie glanced around making sure there was no one else in this part of the garden.

"Ah, so that's it," Hamish ran his hand over the hull.

Annie looked at him sharply.

"Hey, don't worry. I'm good at secrets." He was fiddling with the sails now. "This really is some little beaut."

The swing creaked back and forth.

"Annie," Hamish asked several moments later, "do you think we could take *Bill* out again, maybe now, this afternoon?"

"No need. I've already had him out. He can do anything. It's amazing." Annie sat on her hands and looked smug.

"But how do *I* know that?" He gave her a hard stare.

"You think I'm making it up?"

"No, but did you really make it tough or did you just stay in the safe little rock pools?"

"So what do *you* want to do? Go ripping off with him like before."

"I didn't rip off. Besides that pool was tame as anything." Hamish set *Bill* down on the grass.

"It was not! It was a horrible place."

"Look Annie, what's the sense in having a boat if you don't *really* sail it?" Hamish screwed up his face, pleading.

"You mean unless you take risks?"

"Ah, never mind then. I suppose girls don't like that sort of stuff. They wanna be safe all the time." He dropped his shoulders and he sighed.

"That's not fair lumping me in with 'girls' like that! I've taken plenty of risks."

"Such as?"

She shifted uncomfortably and bit her lip, ignoring his question. But she was getting steamed. "So you're a better person to test *Bill* than me?"

"Yeah, maybe."

"Really?"

"You know, Annie, test pilots push if they wanna

find out what a plane'll do. My Dad said. Same thing with a boat. Don'tya wanna know what it'll do if you're not cuddling it all the time?"

'Cuddling' was the last straw. "Ok, then, smarty pants, *do* it. Take him." There, she'd said it.

"Really? You'll come with me then?" Hamish' eyes were wide.

"Not this time, Hamish, you're on your own. If you think you're such a great test pilot prove it. But I want my boat back in one piece!" said Annie wagging a stern finger at him.

"You mean that? We could go where we sailed him last time. Great place for some interesting manoeuvres. Sure you don't wanna come?"

Annie hesitated. "I can't. I promised Mum I'd go with her to Gran's this afternoon."

"You're sure now?"

"Yes, I told you *YES!* But remember; a full report; everything that happens. You got that?" Her fingers were wagging again.

"Sure. I promise. I just can't believe you're letting me."

Annie wasn't sure she could either. Their conversation had sort of run away with itself but if she took back anything now he'd call her a sissy. "It's okay, Hamish, just go now before I change my mind," and she picked up the box and pushed it right at him.

* * *

In point of fact Annie had been thinking of a plan something like this while she was in the workshop.

She needed Hamish to agree that the *William Morr* was remarkable; that it could sail by itself as though there was someone "on board", steering and adjusting the sails. If he took the boat alone and this happened too, she would know she wasn't crazy. But should she have trusted him?

But why had her boat become so incredibly important, anyway? Was it because she had "rescued" it for Moira; because it made her brave or because its performance on the water seemed miraculous? Could a boat like that *know* it had some special part to play like some talisman that guards a person from harm? Annie's imagination was running free now. That's it, she thought. It is *Moira* that *Bill* is reaching out to; *Moira* who needs protection from that terrifying illness! She'd read books where stuff like this happened and they weren't all fairy tales.

Chapter Nine

Gran's Gift

Annie always looked forward to being with her Grandmother. She made her feel welcome and important and she *listened*. So many adults wouldn't do that; her mother being a great example lately.

And Annie loved her house too. Rose Cottage sat on a cobbled street sandwiched in between a row of ancient stone houses that seemed to lean against each other for support. But unlike the adjoining houses with their plain black window frames, Gran's were shuttered in bright blue. The door was blue too, its wooden boards smoothed and shiny.

Before Annie had a chance to lift the large brass knocker Gran had flung it wide in greeting to them both.

"Annie! Meg dear, come away in now. I've a pot of tea all ready on the stove!"

Inside the tiny house everything was close to everything else. If Annie stood in the middle of the hall her fingertips touched both Gran's bedroom door and the door to the bathroom; then a quarter turn and the kitchen was right there too.

That afternoon Annie and her mother shared the flowered couch in the over-stuffed sitting room, their knees bumping into the coffee table, their feet brushing up against the sewing basket underneath. Gran sat on a swivel rocker by the bookcase, her teacup and saucer on the lamp table opposite. From their faded frames above the fireplace the faces of a gallery of relatives watched over them. Along with pen and ink sketches of the village that Gran had drawn was an embroidered rose in a sandalwood frame. The walls were as crowded as the floor.

*   *   *

The conversation between Annie's mother and Gran moved from problems at the guest house to her father's working hours, from the unusually cool weather to the ridiculous price of eggs and butter. Annie's mind drifted.

"So, what have you been up to, my wee lass?" Gran asked.

"Oh, just the usual stuff." Then realizing that Gran probably *did* care she added, "I'm collecting cowrie shells again to get a head start over Alison in case she comes again this year. I've got almost two hundred already."

"A fine young *gurl*. Such a shame she's only here for a fortnight."

Annie loved the purr of Gran's Scot's brogue. Her mother never sounded like that.

"I wish it was longer too. Still, there's always Hamish."

As soon as the words were out of her mouth Annie regretted it. She knew how much Gran worried about her spending time with him. 'Not a fit companion' she had said more than once and with good reason; a tumble from a sea wall; a collision where both their bicycles rammed one another.

When Annie had come by with both knees bleeding and embedded with small, sharp stones, Gran shook her head. "Did you not see him coming, lass?" How could Annie tell her that they meant to collide just to see what would happen?

Then there was the rabbit episode when they'd nearly buried themselves alive last summer, digging under the edge of the brae; "So it's rabbits, you are then?" Gran shook her head, rinsing the sand from Annie's hair.

Annie thought that was hilarious but she had actually been very frightened when the cave-in started.

"I've chocolate biscuits, lass. Don't be shy now," said Gran changing the subject.

Poor Gran caught between her daughter and her granddaughter, thought Annie reaching for the treat.

"Sandy and I had another letter from the bank about the mortgage payments," said her mother.

Annie excused herself and wandered outside.

* * *

The centre of the back garden was an oval carpet of lush green. Annie kicked off her old pair of too tight sandals and felt the cool, velvety grass between her toes.

She tried a few cartwheels then lay spread-eagled staring up at the clouds floating between the crow-stepped gables and red-tiled rooftops. She saw fantastic shapes drifting across the sky, changing always changing; mystical animals, towering cliffs, boats with billowing sails. Boats! She sat up. How long had Hamish and *Bill* been gone? Several hours at least. Had he noticed anything special about *her* boat after the latest additions?

Restless now, Annie got up and wandered over to the edge of the lawn where a jumble of colourful plants spilled over each other. She looked for the round leaves that Gran sometimes added to her salads. Nasturtiums, Gran told her. She pulled a leaf off one and bit down. The peppery hotness exploded on her tongue. Their flowers looked pretty but weren't as tasty. Then there were snapdragons. She squeezed one or two between her fingers and looked right down inside their striped mouths.

The back door opened. "Are you ready to go, honey? Come and give Gran a hug, then we should be off."

Annie sprinted to the door and wrapped her arms around the elderly woman. "Thanks for the yummy tea. I'll come again soon so we can talk; just the two of us, unless…Mummy, do you mind if I stay with Gran for a bit longer?"

"No, of course not, so long as it's all right with you mother?"

"It'd be grand to have her to myself for a while, Maggie."

"Home by 6 o'clock, Annie, agreed?"

"Agreed."

*   *   *

"Gran," said Annie, once they were back inside and sitting around the remains on the tea tray, "do you believe in magic?"

"Oh now, I don't know about *that*, dearie."

"I'm pretty sure Mummy'd laugh if I asked her and Daddy, well, he prob'ly would too."

"So you think your old Gran, wouldn't, is that right?"

"Well?"

"What I believe is that there are coincidences, lassie; even wonderful ones at times. But such things never come easy. It takes a muckle lot of courage, and determination too."

"Is that a 'yes'?"

"I mean they'll not just happen."

Annie considered this. "D'you think I could do that, Gran? Make something wonderful happen, I mean?"

"It may be. But you are that mysterious. Have you something particular in mind?"

"Well," She searched for the best words to explain things. "I think a wonderful coincidence is happening to me right now. It started when Mummy told me Moira was coming; to get away from that horrible polio thing. You know she's coming, don't you?"

"Indeed I do. We spoke of little else while you were outside. Your mother is very worried about the wee child and for asking for your help. She knows you are a long way from pleased with her right now."

Annie blushed. "You know everything then, don't you?"

"I do."

She gulped and went on. "Well, I was really upset about school but then I got this idea for Moira."

Gran's eyes twinkled. "Go on then, lass."

"Well, I built a boat for her. I'd always sort of wanted one for myself and Moira coming gave me an excuse. Well, actually I *repaired* a boat but I want to keep that part a secret. It was a broken one," Annie hesitated, "in Daddy's workshop."

"Your father doesn't know now, does he?"

"No, not yet. I didn't want to tell him till it was finished. Gran, I spent ages trying to build one of my own, truly I did, but it was hopeless! And just when I was about to give up, well, the *William Morr* sort of fell into my hands."

"And all this time your father was none the wiser?"

"Everyone's been far too busy to notice much of anything *I* do." She hoped Gran wasn't going to disapprove, "The boat was a real beauty but it *was* badly damaged so I thought maybe I could fix it."

"That could not have been an easy task," Gran said slowly.

"It wasn't, but it helped to use Daddy's tools and some other stuff from those little drawers."

"Oh, dear."

"But that's only part of why I want it secret. The other part is how it's turned out. I can't believe something I made, well partly anyway, could be so perfect. This boat can pretty well sail by itself and we've already had some adventures."

"Adventures?" Gran frowned.

Annie shifted directions a bit. "Don't you think Moira will love having *William Morr* to play with?

That's the name on the stern of the boat. But I'm calling him *Bill* so it's easier for her. But the best part is he feels magic. At least I hope he is."

"Then so do I. Lucky Moira to have a cousin who cares so much. And of course it should be a surprise. Let's hope your father will be proud when he sees what you've done."

"Me too." Annie helped herself to the last chocolate biscuit and leaned back into the cushions.

"Oh I nearly forgot, "said Gran, "I have a surprise for you. Look up there on the mantelpiece."

Annie smiled at Gran and reached toward the fireplace.

"Go on take it; it's yours now."

"Is this it?" She picked up a small leather pouch. "It's not been there all afternoon, has it?"

Gran smiled. "Missed it, didn't you, while your mind was off wool gathering?"

"I did!" She untied the string. "Oh, Gran, it's beautiful!" she pulled out a smooth blue stone the colour and shape of a robin's egg.

"I've had this since I was your age, Annie, twelve, the age of wonder. Morag, my Celtic nurse, gave it to me, and I believe she had second sight."

"You mean she could see the future?"

"In a way. You see, it is my belief that sometimes things happen in life that can't be explained by science. Morag was not one to speak about her gift very much but you could tell by looking at her that the world moved round her differently."

"Oh," Annie caught her breath, and smiled.

"She was the kindest person I have ever met," Gran

went on. "I loved her very much and it nearly broke my heart when she died."

Annie's skin prickled.

"Gran are you sure you want to give me this?"

"I always intended for you to have it and now feels like the right time."

Annie turned her new treasure over in her hands, feeling its smoothness, admiring the perfection of its shape. She pressed it to her cheek and said mischievously. "So it's not a piece of the bluestone from outside St. Mary's?"

Gran's teacup rattled on its saucer. "Heaven's no! Why would I give you a piece of the devil's handiwork?"

Annie was very familiar with the old legend. It told how Satan, in a fit of rage, had hurled a huge blue stone all the way from the May Island, ten miles away across the sea. The stone still lay outside the very church he had hoped to destroy. For good luck some superstitious passersby would kiss the small hollow on its edge. It was devil's thumbprint, they said. Annie couldn't imagine who'd want put their lips near the ugly thing!

"Gran, I'm joking."

"You should be very careful making fun like that; disturbing old tales; daring pieces of them to…" Gran stopped. "Oh, Annie, what am I saying? Pay no attention to the ramblings of an old lady."

Annie reached over and took her hand. Gran was such a different person from her mother it was sometimes hard to believe they were related. "Gran, I shouldn't've teased you. I'm sorry. I love my present. It's beautiful. Nothing from that other horrid stone would look anything like this."

The clock in Gran's bedroom struck six.

"Oh, I've got to dash," said Annie jumping up. "Mummy'll be furious if I miss another deadline."

Gran and Annie walked arm in arm to the door. "Goodbye, dear girl," Gran said hugging her, "and come back soon because I do love hearing about your *adventures*."

Chapter Ten

Now What?

Annie was over the moon with this latest addition to her treasure collection.

She had always found stones appealing, looking down whenever she was on a beach to see what might be waiting there. At first the pebbles around her would look quite ordinary then she would see one that wasn't and she'd bend down to find another and another. Her pockets bulged, tore sometimes, but she didn't care.

This one from Gran was amazing, just like the *William Morr* was amazing, and now destiny had brought them together.

And *Bill* and Hamish were still together too. But she shouldn't worry. He'd promised to return the boat that evening and tell her the whole story, whatever it turned out to be. Annie touched the stone in her pocket. Its silky smoothness made her feel less anxious.

*   *   *

But Annie's calm fell all to bits again when she reached home and Aileen said that Hamish had already stopped by.

"But he can't have!"

"He said to tell you he wanted a word wi' you," she explained.

"He knew I was at Gran's. What was he thinking?"

"He didn'a remember you were out. He looked right upset."

Annie's stomach lurched. "Did he bring something for me?"

"No missy, he didn'a have anything wi' him at a' but his sad face."

*　*　*

So where was the boat if Hamish didn't have it? But he probably did though. Even upset as he was, he would hardly have brought it to the door and handed it to Aileen. The evening passed with excruciating slowness as she waited. He'd come back after supper, surely.

To pass the time Annie volunteered for kitchen duty. She scraped dishes and stacked them, dried mountains of pots and pans and helped set the tables again for breakfast. Bozz was underfoot as usual looking for tasty scraps and ignoring the contents of his cat dish because the aroma of grilled mackerel still lingered in the air.

"Yeow… yeow," Bozz kept pushing between Annie legs to hurry her.

Annie checked the plate scrapings for pieces of crisp skin with some meat still attached.

"Yeow… yeow… yeow," Bozz kept up the racket.

"Do be still, it's coming, you silly animal," she murmured and placed a saucer on the floor. "There now; how's that?"

Bozz' tail dropped from the vertical and rested on the tiles. His furry face was surrounded by the fishy treat, his whiskers twitching as he nibbled.

Annie sat at the kitchen table and watched, soothed for the moment.

The evening dragged on. No Hamish. She went back to her latest sailing book. She was still reading the one about the woman who had sailed her boat alone around the world. The gorgeous descriptions of sunsets and moonlit seas enthralled her. So did every electrifying word of the storms she had survived. Annie was staggered by her bravery. Then her concentration would snap. Something must have gone very wrong for Hamish to forget she was at Gran's.

*   *   *

By nine o'clock there was still no sign of Hamish. He wouldn't be coming now. Annie started upstairs for bed.

Then the phone rang. She wondered if it was Hamish at long last though their parents didn't like them to use the phone. You had to drop coins in a meter every time you made a call so it was really only meant for serious communication, not chatter. She crept downstairs to listen. The kitchen door was open.

"No!" came her mother's troubled voice, "Oh, that can't be true Gracie!"

Annie's heart sank. What awful news had Aunt Grace called about? She moved closer and stood in the doorway.

"Oh, my dear, how awful. Where is she now?" Silence, while her mother listened then the clang of another shilling in the meter.

"Right, of course. How long until you know more definitely?...Yes, I'll tell her... Goodbye, Gracie. Give my love to Peter."

The phone clicked back onto the hook. Annie hardly dared move.

"Annie? Is that you, honey? It's all right, come here. I could use a hug."

She walked across the kitchen and wrapped her arms around her mother. "Oh, Mummy, it's Moira, isn't it?"

"Yes, my darling, I'm afraid it is."

*   *   *

The news of Moira's illness was horrible. She had to be rushed to hospital; she was feverish; she was suffering from aches and chills; all the things that happened to someone coming down with polio.

So frightening for a little girl; and she was only six! Could she die? At six? Stupid Annie! Imagine thinking that the magic in her boat, even if there *was* any, could protect Moira. How could she believe such nonsense? Too many books; too many fairy tales.

But then what if *Bill* was lost? Or broken or wrecked? Is that why Hamish had to talk to her face to face? To explain? And how could *Bill* protect Moira when he couldn't even save himself? Could there possibly or impossibly be *any* connection? Gran, *dear Gran*, had said only that afternoon that there were more things in the world than could be explained by science. She had talked about coincidences too; wonderful ones. What if there were horrible ones as well?

In Annie's befuddled brain it all came back to *Bill*. She switched off her bedside light and stared into the darkness of her room. She tossed unable to sleep, her mind whirling with imaginings of disaster until she became convinced of the worst. It didn't matter that Hamish hadn't told her anything. *She knew. Bill* was definitely lost or that terrible phone call from Aunt Grace would never have happened.

Which meant that, somehow, Annie had to find the boat herself; and soon. Maybe even tonight?

Whether for courage or comfort, Annie reached for the blue stone resting on her night table. It felt warm in her hand; odd for a stone. But even more odd was that now, in the darkness of her room, she could still see its rounded blue shape. It seemed to be as alert and wakeful as Annie was.

Then the full moon suddenly moved out from behind its curtain of clouds and bathed Annie's room in light. The stone glowed bluer than ever.

Chapter Eleven

Night Mysteries

It was nearly midnight when Annie finally felt it was safe to step out into the hall and tiptoe downstairs. As she reached the curve in the stairway she could just make out the brass hands of the grandfather clock as they snapped together and pointed straight up. Then came the first ear splitting bong! There would be eleven more and then surely everyone in the house would hear it too, and find her there, shaking in her shorts. She placed her feet ever more softly on each stair leading down to the front hall. Moonlight streamed into the open entrance through the glass side doors making a strange colourless light on the carpet. But Annie couldn't go out that way because the heavy outer doors creaked too much. It would have to be the kitchen door, then, down the dark pathway to the side gate. Gritting her teeth, she lifted the latch and stepped outside.

The back garden was dark; the trees in heavy silhouette. The rising moon had not yet moved above the bulk of the three-storey house. Annie felt the stone warm in her pocket as she moved in haste along the path. She didn't notice the other, blacker shadow that followed and slipped through the gate after her. Annie had almost reached the moonlit crescent that separated her house from the sea when the shadow bumped into her throwing her off balance onto the grass verge.

"Yeow," squealed the shadow.

"Bozz!" yelped Annie. "You scared me to death."

"Yeow," Bozz sounded winded too.

"Out on one of your midnight prowls again, are you, Bozz?"

"Yeow?"

"I'm going down to the beach to find *Bill*. I think he's in trouble."

Bozz gave Annie one of his long, inscrutable stares.

"Aileen told me Hamish was really upset this afternoon and I'm sure that's the reason. So, what do you say, cat? Are you in?"

Bozz sat down on the path and turned to face the house.

"You don't like the idea of the beach, do you?"

Bozz didn't move a whisker.

"I have to go anyway, Bozz. So think about it. It would be nice to have your company though."

A rumbling growl emerged from Bozz' throat.

Annie took this to mean she was on her own. She didn't have time for any more persuasion. She set off firmly, if a bit unhappily, for the dismal and threatening pool where she and Hamish had first sailed the *William Morr*.

The furry shadow hesitated then broke into a trot behind her.

When Annie reached the dark pond the moonlight revealed nothing floating across its surface. Where else might he have gone? She looked around her. The moon was the perfect lamp and made it easy to see sharp rocks, pools and sea weedy patches. She would try further on beyond the next outcropping of rocks where other open pools spilled into the sea.

Annie and a very cautious Bozz wandered on. It was an enchanting night. The shush of the waves mingled with the splashes and soft barks from a pod of seals. Their backs flashed silver as they curved from the water. What had brought them so close to shore?

"It's so different here at night; so beautiful," Annie whispered. "Are you out here somewhere *William Morr*, sailing over a moonlit sea?"

Annie felt pieces of herself melt into the night air. Her head swam with wave-like images, her steps carrying her to very edge of the rocks. She kicked off her shoes and began to wade in. The silvery water lapped over her feet, then her knees. It didn't feel cold at all. She dipped her hands into the water and threw showers into the sky and watched as the droplets shimmered off her fingers. It was like picking up the stars.

With slow steps she moved into deeper water. The ocean lifted her arms up to her shoulders. She let her feet drift off the sand and rise to the surface. She was floating open armed inside the bowl of sea and sky.

"This must be what heaven is like."

"Yeow!" called Bozz.

*   *   *

Time dipped and spilled around Annie like the sea itself. One moment all her senses were alive with sounds and sensations and the next she drifted in a dream of stillness.

"Yeow! Yeow!" Bozz called again from the shore.

She stirred and rolled her body so she could look into the water below. A shaft of moonlight broke through the surface clear to the sandy bottom. Now she could see fish darting about, a lobster whipping its tail and rocketing backwards, and fronds of dark polyp-covered seaweed swaying as the tide breathed. Then, far down caught under a barnacle-covered rock, emerged the familiar shape of a small wooden boat.

"*Bill*," Annie spluttered, wide awake and alert. She stared more closely, her eyes stinging in the salty water.

Every so often the pull of the tide would move *Bill*'s stern up a little then drop it again. A piece of tarred string, likely torn from a fisherman's net, had wound around the boat holding it to the rock.

She blinked. The pictured blurred. Annie took some deep breaths and tried looking down into the sea again. The moon kept changing its mind about the lighting, making it hard to see.

Diving to get him might be possible. The recent memory of being underwater swam back into Annie's mind. She could do it again, surely? After all it was *Bill* down there. Once she got him free they would make it out together.

"Bozz, I'm going down," Annie called.

She had read somewhere that if you want to dive underwater and stay for a while you need to fill your lungs extra full of air. You had to be careful though because there had been something about losing consciousness.

She began taking in great gulps, holding her breath, and then slowly releasing the air. She did this three or four times, feeling her lungs get bigger inside, holding more. On the fifth breath she tucked herself in half then pushed down hard her legs kicking, her arms swimming out for extra power. She felt herself descend but not very far. She burst back up to the surface in a rush.

It was going to take more practice. She rested in floating position before a second attempt. This one was much more successful but still short of her goal. Another rest. The third time she succeeded in touching *Bill*'s side before she ran out of breath.

"Well Bozz, this is it," Annie called to the furry outline sitting on the rocks, "if I don't get him this time I'll be too tired to try again."

On the fourth dive she reached the barnacled rock with breath to spare and began to unwind the tangled netting. *Bill* inched out from his prison.

Just a little more unwinding and you'll be free; her lungs were near to bursting.

It was then the dark shadow came slowly through the water from above. There was still one more piece of line to untangle.

'We can do this, *Bill*, we can,' the words buzzed in her head. But the darkness was right over her now and it didn't move away. It was like a huge net, a great smothering hand touching her face.

*   *   *

Annie felt the stone slip from her pocket. She grabbed for it. But the swirling rush in her head made her efforts too clumsy and the stone tumbled through the water, twisting over on itself as it fell, then came to rest on the deck of the William Morr.

A silvery blue light filled the pool and everything in it froze. Something was changing. The light was doing it; the light from the stone.

There was a quivering hum in the water. Annie felt it buzz and prickle over her skin. Her chest felt tight; her head light and dizzy. There were pictures coming in and out of focus in front of her eyes.

The decks were the first to grow, bursting and splintering through the wood, till a new one stretched forward and aft, port and starboard in long, gleaming planks. The bow rose before her. The hull moved down into the water lifting the whole yacht up and out. From the top deck the tall mast cut the water's surface. The sea streamed down its sides in a silver waterfall. And as the new William Morr broke from his rocky prison he took Annie with him, cradled in his cockpit. Out they sailed together, out into the open sea and over the deep, safe water.

At the very moment the sun crested the horizon the newly minted craft, its sails unfurled, curved into the wind. Annie felt the rush of it in her face and the boat's tiller firm in her hand. Out across the sea they skimmed, the rustle of waves rolling past the bow and creaming off the stern in a frothy wake like whipped milk.

Her cheeks were wet with spray.

"We're finished with the rock pools. It's time to meet the sea," whistled the wind through the billowing sails.

They headed right into the sunrise across a sea of red and

gold. The sky turned lemon pale and the sun rose higher and brighter. The gigantic strength of the ocean pressed against them, its rolling pulse like a heartbeat.

When Annie took her eyes off the sails and looked at the sea it was a deep, rich blue, its surface twinkling with sun pennies. They were nearing an island now. The cries of hundreds of birds spilled off the high cliffs and tumbled over the crashing surf. Annie tacked safely round the rocky shoreline. And there, around the next headland, rose the lighthouse keeper's home. At the top of the tower Annie could see the gigantic headlight, the huge glass face that had winked at her so often across the bay at night.

"Hello there, May Island!" her voice cried into the waves. Now she could tell Tam she'd been far out past the place he fished for mackerel or tossed his lobster pots.

Suddenly the sea boiled with movement. The seals had come back. Their shiny backs arched out of the waves splashing and diving so close that Annie could smell their saltiness and hear their rasping breath. She reached out and for a split second touched the slippery hide of a passing swimmer.

Then abruptly, they vanished. The wind kicked hard and Annie grabbed the tiller with both hands. They were coming out of the lee of the island, heading south, the Bass Rock in their sights.

As the afternoon sun dipped off to the west the Rock and the Island faded from view. Annie was tiring and struggled to hold their speed and course. Bill was too strong for her. She needed to rest.

The shadow of the mast lay long across the deck when they approached the cove.

Chapter Twelve

Red Sky in the Morning

Bozz sat on the shoreline, his tail swaying from side to side, waiting. When Annie called out to him for the last time Bozz moved farther out along the rocky arm, to the edge where Annie had been splashing. The water was calm now. Bozz looked down. Bubbles burst on the water's surface; shadows flickered from below. He dipped a paw into the water then shook it. He didn't like the feeling. He shrank back.

The moon slipped in and out between the clouds.

*   *   *

Bill ghosted under sail into an opening between the high sheltering rocks. The sea wound in around them like a river. After many turns it opened into a cove where the water lapped on a sandy beach hidden from the sea. A few barnacle crusted moorings bobbed on the water. Annie leaned over the side and passed a bow line through one to hold them fast.

Once they were safe from drifting Annie moved up onto the deck to drop the sails. She scooped them around the boom and drew the lines tight. How tired she felt as she lay down on the deck to rest, the shadow of Bill's mast falling across her.

"Never...in all my life..." Annie fought a strange heaviness in her head.

How easy to lie there forever, rocking in the bay's gentle motion. But something urged her to rise. She ran her hands along the warm wood of the deck then let herself drop down, down into the shallow water.

"I'll be back. I promise..." she slipped into the warm waves. She watched the William Morr blur into the distance as she walked toward the beach; such a long way. Her legs pushed on but the sand was no closer and the water grew deeper. No beach now, just rocks; a ledge she had to climb, to get up and breathe.

*   *   *

A breeze freshened to the east and a crack of gold appeared along the horizon giving way to a sudden glory of crimson clouds. Bozz, now tired of waiting for Annie took the roundabout, cat about, route home. He had some favorite corners to snooze in, some walls to jump on, and a rival to hiss at. So, it was conveniently the breakfast hour when he pushed at his cat door and entered the kitchen.

Annie's mother was using the telephone, her voice raised, "Annie isn't with you? What about Hamish? Is he at home?"

Mrs. Mac pushed her hands through her hair. "He is? So they're not together."

Aileen looked anxiously across the kitchen.

"Thanks Jean. No, that won't be necessary. I'll let you know."

Annie's mum sighed and slowly returned the phone to its hook. "She's probably just off on another of her wanders," she said to Aileen who had stopped drying dishes and was staring at her. "I can't understand what gets into her sometimes. She drives me frantic!"

"Dinna worry, madam," said Aileen. "Annie's a smart wee lass."

Mrs. Mac slumped down into a kitchen chair.

"Yeow," cried Bozz, to announce his presence.

"But where is that daughter of mine? Her bed was hardly slept in. She's been gone for hours, Aileen, and at *night*. Oh, just wait till she gets home. She'll have some explaining to do then."

"Ye do encourage her to take care o' hersel', madam," Aileen twisted the tea towel in her hands.

"But in the *dark*, Aileen!" Annie's mother was not to be consoled. "Anything could happen in the dark."

"Yeow!" Bozz crossed the kitchen and pushed against Aileen's legs.

"Awa' with ye, cat! We've more important things to worry about the now than yer breakfast."

"Yeow!" Bozz signaled one more time then darted out the door.

*   *   *

"Who was on the phone, Mum?" Hamish asked then wished he hadn't. He already guessed from half of the conversation that it had been Annie's mother and there was a problem.

"Do you know anything about this?" his mother's tone was sharp.

"Nothing; well, not for sure." Hamish squirmed.

"I'm guessing you know a lot more than anyone else."

So, there would be no beating about the bush. "Annie's not home is she?"

"You've got that right. She's been gone most of the night according to Margaret. Now shoot."

"Well, I borrowed…No, that's wrong, Annie lent me something to test out; something she had made."

"Something to *test*?"

"Yeah. Well, she knew I wouldn't make it easy." This explained nothing but he had to cover for Annie and he knew how adults blabbed to each other.

"Hamish, I'm waiting."

"Okay, I'm getting there. So I was down by the shore rocks testing this thing Annie gave me. I was supposed to take it back after. She *could've* gone looking when I didn't show up."

"Are you suggesting that's where Annie went last night; to the beach?"

"Maybe."

"Ye Gods, Hamish, and she's not home *yet*! Do you know what that means?"

Hamish legs went all rubbery.

"I'm calling Sandy McLeod right now. And you, dear boy, are going to show us exactly where you were yesterday."

* * *

"Margaret, it's me, honey. I'm calling from the Station."

"Oh, Sandy, thank God! Have you heard anything?"

"I just had a call from Jean. Hamish thinks he knows where Annie might be."

"Oh, I knew it. That boy is nothing but trouble!" she burst out.

"It does look like that," said Sandy carefully, "but this time I think he's the one to help. We're going down to the beach to look."

The line went silent.

"Maggie, are you all right? Maggie?"

"I should be there too."

"No, Maggie. I'm taking care of this."

"Of course; I'd probably just be in the way fussing my head off." Annie's mum paced the floor phone receiver in hand.

"Maggie?"

"Sorry, I thought I was going to faint. I'm alright now, I think."

"You sure?"

"It's just…Sandy this is my worst, worst nightmare."

"I know my love; hang on. I'll call just as soon as we know more. If nothing shows up," his voice broke, "I'll call the police."

"Sandy, I've done that already. I thought it was them when the phone rang."

"Where did you tell them to check?"

"Anywhere along the shore; you'll probably see them yourself."

*   *   *

Sandy left the harbour office and drove to the end of Nethergate Street. He pulled in and parked behind two empty police cars and hurried down the lane leading to the seawall footpath. The tide was out. As Sandy rounded the last corner he could just make out the uniformed men walking along the shore to the north lifting mats of seaweed with their sticks, pointing and motioning to each other, their voices out of range. A few holiday makers looked on like silent actors in some frightening play.

Hamish and his mother were waiting for him at the end of the path. From this vantage point they stood in silence scanning the rocks below and off to the south, now fully revealed by the low tide. A couple of village boys were horsing around and yelling to each other. They were near the same wide open pool where Hamish and Annie had first taken *Bill*.

The three made their way down the seawall steps to the rocks and the gurgling stream that poured fresh water back into the sea. There was no beach to speak of there, just rocks.

Hamish glanced nervously at his mother, "This really isn't a good place for you to be, Mum."

"I'm perfectly fine," she answered quickly.

Sandy said, "Jean, Hamish is right. Besides it would be better if we spread out a bit. You stay here near the steps. You could run up and signal to us if you see anything and I'll keep going with Hamish for a bit."

Hamish looked relieved and rubbed some tension out of his back. "Thank you, sir. The rocks are going to be pretty slippery ahead though, Mr. McLeod. Why don't I do the low tide areas and you search back here?"

Annie's dad nodded and Hamish watched him move with surprising agility over some nearby rocks that soon took him out of sight. Hamish turned and picked his own way cautiously over some others that blocked the view of the sea.

Jean Findlay had the worst job; waiting and watching. The moments crawled by like a movie picture that had stalled. Waves lapped with a steady, unchanging rhythm over the flat rocks nearer the sea and the sky was eerily overcast as though in readiness for a storm. Her nerves were stretched almost beyond bearing when she thought she heard Hamish shouting, "Over here! I've found her!" His voice echoed again as he reappeared from a distance waving his arms, "Over here!" She climbed a step or two and was able to see Sandy, in his seaman's boots, bolting towards the waving arm which had disappeared again around a tall stand of rocks.

*   *   *

Annie couldn't have chosen a better place to hide in plain sight if she had tried. When her father rounded the rocks she was just sitting there on a ledge, completely still, staring out to sea.

"Annie!" he shouted, "what in heaven's name are you doing?"

She remained motionless; staring. Her chestnut hair was caught with seaweed that hid some of the gash on her forehead, her bare legs were bruised, her arms webbed with cuts.

"Annie! Can you hear me? Speak to me, for heaven's

sake!" Her father's tanned and weathered face drained of colour.

Then very slowly Annie turned. Her forehead still oozed blood. Her pale blue eyes had a glazed look. She blinked a few times taking it in that she was no longer alone.

Tears started to run down her cheeks and then a huge sob wracked her body.

"Ye Gods, Annie!" her father wrapped his arms around the slender body with the torn blouse and soaking shorts. They rocked back and forth.

"Oh, Daddy, what's happened? Why am I *here*?"

"Annie, it's all right. *I'm* here now and we're going home."

"No, Daddy, I have to stay. I have to find him; all over again." Annie's eyes were pleading.

"Not now, sweetheart, not now; whatever it is can be found later."

Annie started to shiver. She tried to push her father away but she hadn't the strength. Her tears welled up again.

Her father lifted her, still weeping, into his arms. He walked slowly, testing each step back around and across the rocks to where Jean stood waiting, her cardigan wrapped too tightly, biting her lip to keep control of her face. In moments two other policemen appeared with some sort of makeshift stretcher. Annie's father stooped and laid her on it. Her body immediately went limp and her eyes closed. A couple of boys hovered in the distance, staring. The police waved them away.

The officer in charge spoke to Sandy, "Your daughter, sir? Have you any idea what happened?"

"I'm not sure. She's never done anything like this before."

"By the looks of her she may have suffered a blow to her head," the sergeant said. "Better have one of my men get her to a doctor."

"She was just sitting there when we arrived; disoriented, but..."

"We should go now, sir."

"You're quite right. Thank you." There was a pause. "Could someone at the station contact my wife?"

"Of course, sir; no trouble at all."

"Thank you. Thank you so much. You're very kind."

Sandy McLeod and Jean Findlay followed the stretcher as another officer, holding a notebook, approached. "So you found her, sir. Annie MacLeod, isn't it?"

"Yes, my daughter, Annie. But she..."

"Not now, McTaggart," the sergeant brushed him off.

"I'm sorry, Mr. McLeod. It's just that I will have to write a report."

"Perhaps I could answer your questions." Jean said to McTaggart. "Would you like me to come with you?"

"Yes, madam, that would be helpful."

"And my son Hamish too; they were friends. He was the one who found Annie."

The first police van with Annie and her father pulled away, its siren wailing, followed by the sergeant and his men in their car. Only McTaggart remained with Hamish and his mum, taking notes.

Chapter Thirteen

A Long Day

In the police car Annie opened her eyes. She coughed and spat some watery phlegm into her father's handkerchief. At the clinic she said she felt more tired than hurt, but the doctor insisted on a checkup. He took her temperature, her blood pressure, looked into her eyes and waved fingers for her to count. It made her even more tired. She desperately wanted to go home and shut her eyes but even after they discharged her sleeping was not permitted for a few more hours.

"It's very important she stay awake after a head injury," the doctor announced brusquely. Annie groaned.

*   *   *

It was a very long day for Annie, sitting up in bed, forcing herself to read, having Aileen dropping in with her disapproving face to make sure she stayed awake.

"Where's Bozz?" Annie asked, longing for some friendly company.

"No idea, missy." Aileen replied.

"I nearly drowned, didn't I?" Annie muttered to the empty room. "You'd think people would be nicer."

*   *   *

Annie had never known her parents so upset. She could see their strained expressions, hear their quiet words. She wished they would just shout their anger; it would be easier to take.

The day dragged by. She fought to stay awake. Aileen dropped in with maddening regularity to be sure orders were obeyed. Each time Annie turned her back on her. She could hear Aileen' sighs and knew how much the woman wanted to speak her mind.

She lay in her bed staring at the changing patterns of the sunlight and cloud on the ceiling. Late morning became afternoon. The light darted about. The curtains moved in the breeze reminding her of silver waves, cries of the seabirds and the thrill of being at the helm of the *William Morr*.

More time passed. The sunlight was fading. Her room was full of shadows. A rumble of thunder sounded in the distance.

Annie's head still pounded. Her thoughts made no sense. She remembered such beautiful things and such terrifying blackness too. She would just rest a little longer then try to figure it out.

There was a knock on her door.

"Aileen?" Annie peered through drooping eyes.

"Madam says it's alright if you fall asleep now."
Aileen' voice was less edgy than before. "How are you
feeling, missy?"

"Baffed; dying to sleep..."

Annie's eyes closed almost before the door did. She
pulled the covers round her shoulders and melted into
their softness. Then, from somewhere in the distance,
came Gran's voice crooning the beloved Celtic lullaby:

"Vair me o, o roven o… vair me o, o rove a nee,

Vair me o, o ro ho… sad am I without thee…"

*When I'm lonely dear white heart…Black the night or
wild the sea,*

By love's light my foot finds…The old path way to thee."

*   *   *

But when the dreams started they were not sweet
like the song, nor did they bring back the breathtaking
day with the *William Morr*. Something dark crept in…

*They were still at sea but the clouds were gathering. The
wind came in gusty blasts, pushing them off course. The sails
flapped loudly, the boom slammed over and the boat shifted.
Water rushed across her feet as the deck heaved and a chunk
of jagged blue-grey stone rattled across it. Annie's hand went
to her pocket and felt the tear.*

*She clung to the tiller and looked up to the sails for
help. She swung the boat hard but the wind had no gentle
messages for her this time. All forward motion stopped yet
the din of the sails was deafening. She squeezed her eyes shut
and prayed then brought the tiller over slowly, readying for
a port tack.*

Off toward shore grey shapes loomed. Annie watched

*with growing dread as they moved closer, her eyes straining
to keep them in her sights and waited for the wind; nothing.
Her arms and hands ached from holding on. She kept forget-
ting to breathe; she felt light in the head. Steady now.*

*Gradually the outline of the grey shapes grew sharper.
They looked like great cement boxes. They were strung out
along the top of the brae overlooking the sea. She moved the
tiller and the compass needle crept to north-west.*

*But as they turned a blast of wind slammed against
the starboard side whipping the boat clear past her planned
course. The gunnels were in the water; the mast was straining to right itself. She must turn back into the wind. But how
could she when it was everywhere and all around? And all
the while it howled at her: "EASE BACK ON THE TILLER!
RELEASE THE SHEETS! LET THE SAILS GO!!"*

Annie's eyes shot open still clouded with sleep.
She stared out into the room struggling to wake up.
Was she only dreaming the storm? But the rattling of
the windows and the flashes of lightening suggested
otherwise. The thunder rolled and the stone walls of
the house echoed the sound. She slumped back into
exhausted unconsciousness.

*Annie hung onto the tiller for dear life. It was the only
solid thing she had. The rain poured down in buckets; the
deck grew slick; her feet slipped from under her and her
hands let go.*

*Not soon enough. The groaning winch had stretched the
lines to the limit which, unlike Annie, held firm. The sails did
not. Then came a great ripping sound and the mainsail flung
itself out over the sea in yards of useless canvass.*

*Abruptly the boat righted itself and Annie staggered to
her feet. She had to steer somehow but on her life she could*

not see how. The mountainous waves were pushing the boat further into shore; the rocks ahead were high, huge and bristling with sharp edges.

Surfing the wave crests, they skimmed below the huge looming stone blocks with their gaping slits; places where guns once fired on enemy ships! The sound of the storm and the flashes of lightning now cracked like artillery fire!

There was a groaning, more cracks and an earsplitting crash as the mast tore out of the deck. The next wave hissed over the pole of gleaming wood. With no hope of control the wind whipped them toward the rocks and into the narrow opening before them. They rolled and crested into the passage where towering boulders tossed the waves upward and where caves, like great black mouths, sucked the sea inside.

"ANNIEE! YOU MUST JUMP, howled the wind in frenzy.

Annie rolled over in bed. No, she couldn't leave him.

"ANNIE, YOU DID IT BEFORE…JUMP! BEFORE IT'S TOO LATE!!"

Then the wave swept in taking her with it.

*   *   *

Annie's room was in total darkness when she woke again. She turned and groaned. Was this how her adventure had ended and not with *Bill* safely moored in his protected cove?

She rose shakily from the warm cocoon of bedclothes and walked to the window. The glass bent and shook in the gale. Flashes of lightning zigzagged across the sky; thunder echoed more distantly now.

Thirsty and needing to use the bathroom Annie

tiptoed across the hall. She turned the tap and let it run warm holding her hands in the comfort of it. She rubbed the lavender scented soap into foam.

Realizing she was hungry too she made her way down to the kitchen. She snapped on the table lamp. There was a plate of shortbread biscuits on the counter which she thought would be nice with some milk. She poured a little into a glass then sat at the table in the window with the bottle beside her. The rain poured down the panes like tears. Then, from the hallway outside the kitchen came the anxious voices of her parents.

"I *have* to be down there tonight, Margaret. I need to see that the cutter and the lads are ready to go out if we get any calls."

"But *you* won't go out there, will you, Sandy?"

"I'll be monitoring the radio. It'll be the crew that goes out." Her father's tone was clipped.

"I won't sleep, you know. Maybe I'll go and make myself a cup of tea."

"Do that. I'll be back as soon as I can."

The side door closed. Annie heard her mother's slippered steps move toward the kitchen.

She started in surprise when she saw the light was on. "Annie? You're up again?"

"The storm woke me, I think. Daddy's gone out, hasn't he?"

"He has," her mother let the silence hang between them. "You're keeping up your new hours, I see," she said, her eyebrows rising.

"I've not eaten all day. My tummy felt empty."

"So was your bed last night." The lamplight caught a face lined with worry and lack of sleep.

"I'm sorry, Mummy," Annie bowed her head. "I didn't mean to worry you."

"Didn't mean to worry me! What did you think I'd do?"

Here it comes. Annie steeled herself for the blast. "I don't know. I suppose I thought I'd get back before you found out."

"So this was a planned excursion?" Her eyebrows shot up again.

"That's not what I meant. I just had to go. You don't understand." Annie slumped over the table.

"You are right about that. However, I want you to understand something *very* clearly. Your father and I do not want you leaving this house after dark, ever! Is that clear?"

"But, Mummy, that isn't fair!" Annie sat up again.

There was anger in her mother's voice now. "We were distraught. We can scarcely believe you'd do something so foolish. You fell into the sea, Annie. You could have drowned!!"

"But I didn't."

"Not this time." It was a whisper.

Annie remembered the falling but somehow it had a lovely ending her mother could never imagine; the moonlight, the sunrise, the ocean, the whole glorious experience before returning safe to the cove. But then it got muddled. She'd been in her father's arms but not at the cove. Then where? If they didn't find her at the cove had she even been there? She picked up her empty glass to keep her hands steady.

"How did you find me?" she asked, dreading the answer.

"Hamish took Daddy down by the channel rocks, where he thought you'd fallen in."

"Are you sure that's where?"

"Of course I am. Hamish said he'd lost something of yours down there. He thought maybe you'd gone there to look."

"So not at the cove?"

"What cove? There are dozens of them."

So they hadn't found her with *Bill*. Maybe there *was* no *Bill*? No *magical Bill* anyway, to protect Moira and all these wonderful happenings were just her wild imagination? Her chest heaved.

"Darling, you're safe home now." Her mother, relenting a little, walked behind Annie's chair. Her arms reached round her daughter's hunched shoulders, rocking her. "Please don't cry. I've cried enough for both of us."

"It's not that, Mummy. It's not that at all."

* * *

The morning sun had risen and lay across Annie's pillow. She stirred and sat up. The whole room was alight. Even her shelves of sea glass and stones glistened.

Stone! The bluestone! That was the key. If she could hold Gran's lovely gift she would know whether *Bill* was safe. Now, where had she put it? It had been in her pocket when she left the house.

Annie rummaged through the hamper of damp and salty clothes. Good thing Aileen hadn't taken it from her room yet.

"I put it in my shorts pocket, I know I did. It's got to be here." Her trembling fingers felt around the inside of the pocket. She felt a small tear. The seam had parted. The pocket was empty.

"I can't have lost it!" On hands and knees she ran her hands under her dressing table; her bed; anywhere that had a space that a stone, once dropped, might roll.

*   *   *

It was very clear to Annie that her parents were deadly serious about keeping her close to home. Between herself and Moira there had been more than enough to alarm them.

She brought up the subject of Moira when she went down for breakfast.

"Have you been talking to Auntie Grace again?" she asked.

Her mother looked grim. "Moira is in hospital. She is feverish and in some pain. The doctors are doing tests. The only good news is the results are not conclusive."

"What does that mean, exactly? Not conclusive." Annie pushed a sliver of toast into her boiled egg.

"It means that they are not certain Moira actually *has* polio." She had her fingers entwined, prayer-like. "It could be something less serious. But under present circumstances nothing can be overlooked."

"Oh, that's wonderful!" Annie put down her spoon. "Then maybe I still have time!"

"Time for what, for heaven's sake?"

The sarcastic tone in her mother's voice startled her.

"I don't think I want the egg, Mummy."

"All right then. But don't tell me later that you're hungry."

Her fussiness had given her mother another reason to be angry. But that would be nothing compared to her anger if she found out what Annie hoped to do next.

Chapter Fourteen

What Cove?

The plan was to return to the cove where she had left *Bill* after their glorious day together; where tied to the mooring in the fading afternoon sun they drifted, sheltered and hidden by high rocks around them. It was desperation that drove Annie to believe it was the only logical place to look and an even wilder hope that finding him would save Moira.

The problem was which cove and where? She had absolutely no memory of walking home from anywhere. Crumbs, maybe the only way to get there would be by boat. She'd talk to Hamish. He went everywhere on his bicycle and probably knew every cove for miles around and the pathways or fields to get there. The lucky duck would often disappear for an entire day and his mum wouldn't worry. What wonderful freedom!

Annie was also dying to know what had gone on with *Bill* two afternoons ago. Really, was it only two?

*   *   *

"Pss't… Annie. Can you hear me?" The voice was urgent.

She spun around to see Hamish's face through the glass panel in the side door.

"Can you come out?" He looked more untidy than usual.

Annie steadied herself against the kitchen table for a moment. Darn those dizzy spells, then she slipped out the door.

They met at the swing in the west garden. The wind was still blowing strongly and the garden was littered with branches and leaves. The flower pots outside the dining room window had tipped over spilling soil and broken stems on the flagstones. Annie retrieved a fallen pear and wiped it on her shorts. Maybe she should have eaten that egg for breakfast.

"Wow, Annie, am I glad to see you!" He eased himself carefully onto the swing. "How *are* you? You don't *look* too bad apart from that." Hamish pointed at a particularly nasty bump on Annie's forehead.

Annie's hand moved to cover the bruise. "This is nothing, really. But I was pretty shaken up." Annie flopped down on the swing then bit into her pear.

"I bet! Thought you were a goner!"

"Maybe it'd be better if I was."

"You don't mean that!"

"'Course I don't. But things are pretty bad around here. They're watching every move I make. I'll never be able to get away."

"Back up a bit. You've lost me."

"Daddy's been too upset to talk to me. I wanted to go and visit Gran but Mum says I am absolutely not to go worrying her. I hate that. I need to talk."

"You can talk to me."

"I know. Thanks. Dealing with Mum's been the worst though." She took another bite of her pear. "All these rules! She won't let me do anything."

"Poor you. My mum's kinda steamed too."

Annie pulled her jacket round tighter against the wind. "Mum said I'd 'betrayed their trust', or something like that. It's all a big mess. It's not what I planned at all." She kicked at the frame of the swing.

"They'll get over it. They just need more time."

"So do I. Time away from here, to figure things out."

"So? What happened, Annie?"

"No, no. You first. You haven't got Bill, have you?"

Hamish shifted on the swing. "Well, actually, no. That's what I came over to tell you before all this other stuff happened."

"I had that pretty much worked out."

Hamish' voice was low and heavy with apology, "I am *so* sorry, Annie. But I can explain. It wasn't what *I'd* planned either, you know."

"I suppose not. I should never have just handed him over like that."

"Then so much for trusting *me* in future," his head drooped.

"But I'm going to anyway. I need to, Hamish, if…

But that can wait. So tell me; what happened? Every little detail," Annie said pitching her pear core into a nearby bush and turning her full attention on Hamish.

"Okay, if it'll make you feel better." He cleared his throat. "It started off pretty well, actually. We were having a great time. We went over to the stream that leads into the channel under the sea wall. You know the place? Yeah, of course, you would, wouldn't you?"

"We'll get to *me* later."

"Well, anyway, I sailed him down the channel a few times. It winds around a fair bit before it gets to the sea. It seemed like a great test except that on the last trip he got away from me. The channel leads right down to the sea, Annie, right *into* the sea. Oh; sorry."

"It's okay."

"I couldn't believe it. It all happened so fast. He was gone."

"I know. He's incredibly fast."

"Yeah, the current picked up. He was just swept away."

"So, it was the current, you think."

"Of course, what else could it be?"

"You don't think…" She stopped. Nothing Hamish had said sounded the least bit out of the ordinary.

"But that's not the worst of it. I ran like the blazes to catch up to him; then I fell. Wham on the rocks, right on my behind! I didn't want to tell you that part, but I promised not to keep secrets. Besides it still hurts to sit down." He rubbed his tailbone and shifted on the swing.

"Poor Hamish, you really had a beastly day."

"Crickey, nothing like yours! You must've spent

the whole night on those rocks. You've got the bruises to prove it!"

"Yeah. But it wasn't like that for me," Annie said brushing off his concern.

"Well? Do I get to hear your story?"

The back door creaked open. "Annie! Annie, where are you?"

She would have to be stone cold deaf not to hear the worry in her mother's voice.

"I'm on the swing, Mummy, talking to Hamish. Okay?"

"Why are you out there in all this wind? Have you something warm on?"

"See what I mean?" Annie whispered.

"You're staying *in the garden*, aren't you? I don't want you going *anywhere*, is that clear?" The message was crystal clear!

Annie sighed. "I hear you. I'm warm and I'm staying."

The kitchen door slammed again.

"Hamish, I'm not sure where to start. Something's happened to *Bill*, but I don't think you'll believe it."

"Try me."

"Okay; here goes. After you lost sight of *Bill* he must have got swept out to sea."

"I guessed that. But what makes *you* think so?"

"Don't interrupt. This is hard enough."

"Sorry."

"So, I'm guessing once he sailed out there he got caught in a bit of floating net. Then the tide turned and he was swept back in."

"How do you figure that?"

"I'm getting to it. The netting got tangled in the rocks somehow and dragged him down. He was totally trapped."

"And you saw all this?"

"I did, actually." Another flash of that scene flitted in front of her eyes. She shook her head and it went away.

"Are you okay, Annie?"

"Yeah; it's nothing."

Hamish couldn't stop himself, "And I suppose you dived down and saved him, then went for a sail together and came home the next morning!"

"You're mean! You make it all seem stupid and childish and it wasn't that way at all!"

"Hey! Hold on a minute." He stopped the swing with his foot and stared. "You aren't saying all that stuff really happened, are you?"

"I don't know, Hamish. Maybe the whole thing was a dream, but I didn't dream the police or the chewing out I got from my mother."

"Whoa, Annie, I'm sorry. It just sounds really far out, you know."

"It is."

"So what's next?" He looked straight at Annie.

"I take you to *Bill*; the new amazing real life *William Morr*; in the cove where I left him?"

"Wait. Hold on a sec," Hamish held up both hands

Annie ignored the gesture. "*...if* I left him there, that is."

Hamish let out a breath, "So then; you don't believe this either? That's a relief."

"But I do; I think. I'm just so confused." She rubbed

a kink in the back of her neck and squeezed her eyes open and shut a few times. "I thought I left him at Smuggler's Cove, or one of those coves out there." She let out a long breath. "Thing is, I don't remember walking home from there."

"No kidding. We found you here, at the beach."

"I know," she sighed. "It's crazy. I thought we tied up to a mooring and I walked home. Then I have these horrible pictures in my head that I wrecked the boat somewhere else because of the storm."

"Ooo-h, creepy. There was a bad storm; but it was last night, not the night before."

"You see. There are all sorts of real parts. How am I supposed to know which is which? What should I *do*, Hamish?" She twisted a strand of hair in her fingers. "I'm sure *Bill*'s out there somewhere. I think something awful's happened to him. Will you help me find him? Please?"

"Oh, brother; it'll be like looking for a needle in a haystack. You can't possibly expect to find something as small as a model boat somewhere up the coast miles from here."

"Not my *model*, Hamish, the big one; the one he turned into."

Hamish stood up. "You've lost it, Annie, you really have."

"I'm beginning to think so too. But I can't help it. My stomach is turning in circles; I start breathing fast; my head spins and all the time something is saying to me 'find him, you must find him!'" Annie paused for breath. "You're not leaving, are you?" Annie grabbed at his arm. "Please? We can go there together."

"Your parents will tear me to pieces if I take you anywhere near a beach." He sat back down on the swing. "Look, give me a minute, will ya. Let me think."

"So it won't surprise you that my mum thinks you're the reason I got into this trouble," Annie said with a grin; back to her normal self again.

"Now *that's* not fair!" He gave her an aggrieved look.

"No need to shout." She shifted away a bit, "but, in a way, she's right. If you'd brought *Bill* back none of this would've happened."

"Hey, wait a minute!"

"But that's okay. I'm not sorry that you helped. I just wish ..."

Hamish rubbed at his ears; a sure sign he was thinking. "Okay then. What's next *this* time?"

"Well, what about finding a few coves?" Then Annie hesitated. She wasn't sure how to describe the cove. Should she be looking for the peaceful, sunny one or the horrid place where the storm took them? "Do you know of any that have gun bunkers overlooking them?" she said deciding to get the bad choice over with first.

"You mean machine gun emplacements? Also called pill boxes."

"Show off."

"There's a few along the coast; built during the last war. The German subs were right here, you know. The enemy could have got ashore anywhere. Those guns would've blown them out of the water if they'd tried." He held his arms out, operating his machine gun. "RAT-TAT-TAT-TAT!"

"Yes, I know that, but are there any above a cove where a boat could tie up?"

"Maybe; a couple anyway. One 'bout three miles from here; another a mile or two further. That's a pretty rough guess. An hour to an hour and a half, tops, on our bikes'd get us there plus time to check things out; no problem."

"No problem? And what about my imprisonment? Are we going to leave a cardboard cut-out of me on this swing?"

"Hmm," Hamish grinned, "We'd need to leave something in your bed too; in case we're late!"

It was good to laugh again.

The back door opened, caught in the wind and banged. "Annie! Hamish! Are you two still out there?"

"I should go in now. Mummy's getting in one of her states."

"Annie! It's going to rain again; I want you inside; *now*!" She stood at the door, hands on hips.

"Coming! Just one more minute." She turned to Hamish. "I'll think up some bright ideas; you do the same. Come back first thing this afternoon, okay?"

"I'll be here." He gave Annie two thumbs up then walked stiffly to the gate one hand pressed against his sore behind.

Chapter Fifteen

A Tangled Web

After Hamish left, Annie sat at her attic room desk making plans. Her mother thought she was resting. If she only knew!

She pulled out a sheet of paper and started writing. Her ideas kept taking her down blind alleys. It reminded her of A.A. Milne's poem about the sailor who lived on an island. It began:

> *'There once was a sailor my grandfather knew*
> *Who had so many things that he wanted to do*
> *That whenever he thought it was time to begin,*
> *He couldn't because of the state he was in.'*

She stared at the blank page and wrote: *Think of a way to escape.*

In school Miss Sinclair taught that the trick to 'brainstorming' was to write down whatever came into your head no matter how crazy it sounded. In the end these ideas would lead to amazing solutions you'd never have thought of otherwise. So, here goes: HOW? Annie leaned into the page and began scribbling.

1. *Leave a "body":* (But she and Hamish had already thrown that idea out.)

2. *Offer to go on some errand that takes a while:* (That would get her out, maybe, but not back in time before her parents got frantic.)

3. *Persuade Mummy to let me go with Hamish.* (Fat chance)

She fidgeted in her chair. She needed Bozz to help her; they always talked things through together. "Oh, Bozz. I need help. Have you got any brilliant pussy cat thoughts?"

No answer.

Where was that darn cat, anyway? He better not be up on a shelf in the workshop! Come to think of it she hadn't seen him since their night on the beach. The thought of anything else in her life being missing right now was too much; first school and all her friends, then *Bill* and the bluestone and now Bozz.

"I can't stand this! I can't go looking for everything at once," she wailed and stamped around kicking her foot into anything that came into reach, bedpost, waste basket, laundry hamper. The last was her closet door.

There was a scuffle and a squeak and out of the cupboard, at lightning speed, streaked a tiny mouse.

Annie froze; her bad temper over. She had never thought of her closet as a home for mice. Could there be a whole family in there? She pulled the hangers aside, first one way then the other, to let the light reach the floor. There were slippers, sandals, a pair of dirty socks, a couple of grey tennis balls, a skipping rope dangling from a peg, and dust bunnies but no more mice. She stooped to pick up the socks swiping with them at the worst of the dust before dropping them in the empty hamper.

And there it was at the very bottom. The blue stone! "Hallelujah!" She grabbed her robin's egg treasure. It was not going to escape again. She would sew it in.

In the middle of her clumsy stitching the escape solution hit her. If she hadn't been fuming over Bozz it might never have come to light. Good old Bozz.

* * *

By the time Annie and Hamish met again in the afternoon, the entire town was shrouded in fog. The low cloud mass rolled in off the sea hiding the houses, the street and brae below under a grey blanket that muffled sound and made secrets of familiar places. The moaning of the foghorn was the only voice in an eerie landscape that oozed mystery.

Annie kicked her heels against the wall they were sitting on. "I came up with an idea," she said. "Bozz helped."

"Really?"

She plunged in talking a mile a minute.

Hamish interrupted. "Not your Gran?"

"So what's wrong with that?" Annie smiled at the fuzzy outline that was Hamish. She loved the fog.

"You're not supposed to tell her anything, you said, about your, uh, accident."

"I'm not going to tell her about *that*!"

"Okay, then explain." Wincing a bit, Hamish adjusted his perch on the wall.

"I'm going to con Mum into letting me spend a whole day with her. I'll make Bozz part of the reason. I haven't seen him since the night on the beach. It is just possible he's moved in with Gran. There's always a dish of something on her back step. Bozz knows that."

Hamish let out a long breath. "I dunno. You're gonna get your Gran in a pile of trouble."

"Not if we play our cards right," Annie said, her voice bright with determination.

Hamish did not answer.

"So do you have a better idea?" Annie pressed.

Another silence, then a grin on his face.

"Hamish, what are you thinking?"

"Well…" he turned his cap around in his hand.

"What?"

"Maybe I could go out *for* you?"

"Uh- uh! This is my adventure. You're not taking over a second time."

"Seriously. You give me all the dope and I'll report back. It'll be fun and safer too."

"For you maybe. And what am I supposed to do? Just hang around?" Annie gave Hamish a none-too-friendly scowl.

"Okay, okay; let's get back to your plan."

"I'll have to start with Mummy," Annie said, her enthusiasm restored. "She's the biggest hurdle."

*   *   *

"But why *couldn't* I stay a whole day with Gran?" asked Annie, wiping a smudge off the window glass. The fog was lifting.

Annie had cornered her mum writing in her menu plan book. Pages with the headings BREAKFAST, LUNCH, AFTERNOON TEA and DINNER had lines of writing below each with detailed ideas for each meal. Guests at *Lin Cove* certainly had their stomachs well taken care of. Annie's was growling already. She tore her eyes away. "Maybe Bozz is with her," Annie pressed. "If not we could look together. *You* don't have time for stuff like that."

Her mother didn't bite. "Oh, I don't know. It just sounds like too much for an old lady," she answered distractedly and scribbled on.

"She's not an old lady! And she'd love a good walk."

"I know."

Annie embroidered her point. "And she loves Bozz too. She'd want to help, I know she would. And I could help her weed the garden; or carry groceries," she held her breath, sensing her mother might be about to cave.

"Yes, I suppose you could." She put down her pen. "Gran might appreciate that; and your company. It's true I don't get over to see her often. And I *am* very sorry about Bozz, Annie. With all that's going on I just hadn't noticed."

"So can I?"

"Well..."

"Say, yes. There's nothing to do around here since the beach is out of bounds. I'm so bored!"

"Well you know who to thank for that rule, don't you?"

"I know." Then Annie laid it on extra thick. "Helping Gran would sort of be making amends, wouldn't it? I can cycle over right now and tell her; the fog's pretty well cleared."

"You're a persuasive little person, Annie, and I'm a busy one. Go on and see her then. But put on a fresh pair of shorts, please. You've been wearing that same grubby pair for days." Her mother bent over the menus again.

"Thank you *so* much, Mummy." Annie said kissing her mother's cheek to seal the deal. "You won't be sorry."

Chapter Sixteen

Poor Gran

Annie propped her bicycle outside Gran's door, hesitating before knocking. She was about to start a ball rolling that would be hard to control.

Gran loved and trusted her and she would hate to spoil that. Should she tell Gran what had actually happened, whatever that was, or why her parents were so anxious? But if she did that might her grandmother side with them instead?

Annie banged the brass knocker a couple of times. When Gran appeared she was pulling off her garden gloves and had set a wicker basket of flowers beside her in the hallway.

"Well good gracious, Annie! When did you arrive? Have you been knocking long?"

"Not really."

"The peonies were falling over after the rain so I had to cut a few for indoors." She raised the basket of dripping blooms towards Annie's face. "They smell lovely, don't they?"

"M-m-m."

"But come away in out of the damp. I'll put on a kettle and we can talk. It's a lovely surprise to see you."

Annie followed Gran into her tiny kitchen, her mind racing to find the best way to open the difficult conversation. "By the way," she said finally, "Bozz isn't paying you one of his visits is he? He's not been around for a couple of days."

"No, dear, he's not; at least not *in* the house. But if it's only been a day or two I shouldn't worry. You know how cats are. He'll be back when he's ready.

"I know. Just hoping. It's just that too many things are disappearing lately."

"What do you mean, dear?"

"Here let me get that for you," Annie played for time. She reached into the cupboard for the tea caddy and passed it to Gran. Her pots of tea were scrumptious. She had no idea what was in these dried brown leaves; something fruity, something spicy with a tang and sweetness quite unlike the "grownup" tea served at home.

"There's a tin of shortbread biscuits up there too, if you like."

Annie put them on the tray along with Gran's quaint, teapot, cups and saucers and carried it all into the sitting room. A fire burned cheerily in the grate and the heady sweetness of the peonies Gran had placed in a vase on the mantelpiece filled the room. Despite her disappointment about Bozz, Annie was feeling better already.

* * *

"Gran you may not like what I am going to say."

"I'm a might worried already, lass." She placed her cup carefully on its saucer.

"I need you to help me play a trick to outsmart Mummy."

Gran cleared her throat. "Oh, dear."

"I know. I've thought about this a lot and you are my only hope."

"Deceptions are hard on an old lady." She returned her cup and saucer to the tray. "My memory isn't what it used to be."

"Oh, Gran, I love you!" Annie jumped up and threw her arms round her.

"I haven't agreed to anything, dear girl, so don't go buttering me up."

Annie sat back down and started again. "Some really different things have happened to me since I last saw you. Remember the boat of Daddy's I told you I repaired?"

"Of course I remember. You were so happy about the way it sailed." She smiled. "A bit of magic was in it, as I remember."

"It really *is* different, Gran. It has made me do things I never thought I'd do. It's made me brave. But more important is this strange feeling I have that *somehow* the power in that boat is going to help Moira."

"And how could that be, dear one?"

"I fixed it up for her to play with; but I told you that already. She was supposed to come here to be safe from all the sickness."

"And now she can't be here because she is already ill." Gran rubbed her brow.

"I know." Annie continued. "It's so horrible. But there is still a chance. The doctors aren't positive she has *polio*? Not yet; right?"

"That is our hope, but there's not much more we can do right now, other than hope."

"But that may not be true. I know this sounds really weird but while I was mending the boat, Moira was well. But then I lost it Gran."

"Oh, no; I'm so sorry."

"And that was when Moira got sick."

"What a horrible coincidence, my dear."

"Yes, it is." Annie ran her finger around the rim of her cup. "So do you think it's possible that Moira's illness might not be too serious yet?"

Gran sighed. "Well, that's really beyond me to say."

"But don't you see; if there's still time and I can get him back, the *William Morr* I mean maybe…" Her hands were clenched tightly, "maybe it will mean Moira can come back home too?"

"Oh, my dear, would that it were so easy."

Well, perhaps not that easy, Annie thought then went on. "We had such wonderful times and now I've lost him and I'm afraid it's all over; maybe for Moira too."

"No, no, you mustn't say that." A deep intake of breath made Gran's chest heave.

They let the silence hang between them for a long moment.

Finally Gran asked, "And how did you lose the boat?"

"I'm not sure exactly." She let out another long sigh. "I let Hamish borrow it the last day I was here with you," she paused, "and it got away from him and washed out to sea."

"Well then…"

"You're saying it's my fault, aren't you, Gran."

"I'm not surprised, that's all. But I *am* sorry."

"But you mustn't be. You see when Hamish didn't bring him back I went out myself to look. And here comes the bad part. I went at night down to the beach and, and I wasn't home by morning."

"Oh, Annie," Gran said, her face creased with worry.

"Mummy and Daddy called the police. But it was Hamish helped them find me," she rushed on.

"Margaret never said a word about this." Gran laid her hand on her chest. "Heavenly days, child, they must have been beside themselves."

Annie wondered if she should go on. "Are you alright?"

"It's a lot to take in one dose. There's more though, isn't there?" She reached for her teacup and took a sip.

"Yes, a lot. You see it all has to do with what happened that night at the beach. It may have been a dream, I don't know, but in it the *William Morr* and I sailed all the way over to the May Island and The Bass Rock. If it was a dream it was the kind you never want to wake up from. And in the end I left him, safely moored in a cove just past the headland."

"That *is* a lovely tale." Gran's face relaxed into a smile for a moment.

"Yes, but it isn't over. I feel it so strongly. And if I do nothing; if he stays lost I'm terrified that Moira will be too; that she won't ever to come back to us either.

"You are frightening me too, dear girl."

Annie squeezed her palms together. "I'm sorry, Gran. I just can't keep them separate any more. What happens to *Bill* seems all mixed in with Moira."

"Annie, what are you trying to ask me?"

"I want to go back to that cove and find him."

"Annie, no."

"But I have no idea where it is," said Annie ignoring Gran's objections. "You see Daddy and Hamish say they found me on the rocks below the seawall but I honestly don't remember that either. I may have banged my head or something. It's all so muddled." A log shifted in the fire and flared up briefly.

"I don't know what to say." Gran passed her hand over her brow again.

"And there's still more. In another part of my mind *Bill* and I got caught in a storm." Annie was on her feet, pacing to relieve her agitation. "We were thrown up on the rocks and he was wrecked; in another cove, I think, not too far from here. But I don't know if that's true, or if anything at all is true. I just have to get there and find out; I have to."

"Oh my goodness, is there not some other way?"

Annie left her question hanging. "I worry about the things I've seen. Is there something wrong with me?" She sat down again, closer to Gran, looking into her kind grey eyes.

"You must never think that. Dreaming or 'seeing' as you have described to me is a gift, but one that is hard to live with. You have to learn how to live around it, if you know what I mean."

"I think I do."

She reached out for Annie's two hands and held them tight. "I have to tell you that when I was a child I saw things too. Not the way you do but, of course, things were different then."

"Mummy would never say the things you do."

"No, I don't suppose she would. Margaret is a very practical person. Always busy. Maybe she misses things because of that." The old woman's hands left Annie's and smoothed the flowered material of the apron that lay across her lap.

"I love to talk to you, Gran. You make me feel you understand; or want to anyway. And when you gave me the blue stone it became a part of all of it too. I think you knew it would."

There was an awkward silence.

"I had it with me the night I went to the beach. It seemed to be leading me there."

Gran shifted in her chair.

"What's wrong?"

"I just, I just hope giving you the stone was not a mistake, that's all."

"Oh, no, it couldn't be. I keep the stone in my pocket all the time. I'm keeping it safe the way you told me to. I even sewed it in. That way I can't lose it. When I touch it I think *Bill* knows I'm trying to reach him. Does that make sense to you?"

"I think so, a little. It does to you?"

"Most of the time; yes. But the frightening things; the parts I don't want to see that may be connected to Moira…" Annie stopped. Her chest felt tight.

"Oh, Annie I am afraid I have started something

with the stone; with my old lady fancies, and now I can't help you."

She could not have wished for a better moment. "Yes, you can; but will you?"

The question hung in the air. Poor Gran caught in the middle again between daughter and granddaughter. Then she said so quietly that Annie wasn't sure she had heard. "What is it you want me to do?"

"I want you to tell Mummy that I'm spending the whole day with you tomorrow." She cleared her throat, "What you mustn't say is that it's so Hamish and I can find the cove."

A log shifted in the fire. "No, Annie. Not Hamish. Why do you need to involve him again?"

"Because he knows places. And we both have bikes and can go together. Isn't it safer with two?"

"Oh, Annie, I know where your heart is but you are asking me to take on a lot, lying to your mother."

"I know. It sounds like a very bad thing, but if you don't I'll have to do something anyway. At least this way you'll know in case I get into trouble."

"Making ropes out of sand might be easier than what you are asking of me, lass. Let me think. A little more water for my tea, please dear."

Annie poured from the last drops from the pot and waited.

"I will call your mother and let her know if, *and only if,* I decide to go along with this idea," she said, finally.

Annie swallowed. It was very hard on Gran. "You promise me you won't tell her what we talked about?"

"I would only do so for one reason, my dear. And let's both hope it never comes to that."

Chapter Seventeen

When the Fog Clears

The fog was back again the next morning. When Annie came down for a quick breakfast her father wasn't there.

"Is Daddy still at the station?"

"I'm afraid so. He'll be exhausted when he gets home. He's hardly had any sleep for the past two days," her mother sighed. She had the broken parts of the vacuum cleaner plug on the table and she was trying to piece it together.

"Have you spoken to him this morning?"

"No, Annie. I can't bother him when he's so busy, but I certainly would like to, when things like this break down." She glared at the plug.

"Then I don't suppose you know if there have been any distress calls, do you?"

"I have no idea. Why do you ask? There have been storms before. Why the sudden interest?"

"No, it's nothing. I'm sorry to bother you. Um; you haven't seen Bozz yet, have you?"

"No Annie, no Bozz, no distress calls. Now really, dearest, I have a lot to do." She kneeled down again beside the old Hoover and began re-connecting the plug to the end of the cord.

"That's okay. I can check for him around here again; then I'm off to Gran's."

"In all this fog?"

*   *   *

"Bozz!" Annie called through the foggy garden. "Bo...zz!" She tried a few breathy whistles but they didn't carry very well. "Come on, Bozz, you've got to be out there *somewhere*!" She crossed the road and peered down through the fog. No cat on the brae either.

"Here, Bozz, Bozz, Bozz." It was dumb looking for a cat in this weather. He would come home when he blooming well felt like it. Cats were like that.

*   *   *

Truth to tell Annie loved the fog. She was thinking how perfect it was to be returning to her secret cove on a day like this. Together she and Hamish would find *Bill* covered in mist and looking more magical than ever. She could just imagine Hamish's disbelieving face taking in the sheer size of him. The fog would make it all appear more possible; like a dream taking shape right in front of them.

Pedalling up the street was like cycling inside a dream too. She had to be careful though, the pot-holes were hard to see until she was almost on top of them and the fog lights from the oncoming cars startled her.

"I hope they can see me," she said aloud and swerved onto the shoulder to keep out of the way.

*   *   *

Hamish was waiting for her at the crossroads as planned. He was bent over his back tire busy with a bicycle pump. "I hope this old tube holds up over all the bumps," he said, sounding frustrated.

"Cheer up, old boy," said Annie pulling up and hopping off her bike. "It's a great day for an adventure." When he didn't answer she said, "You don't think the fog will make it too hard to find the cove, do you?"

"Nah; this should lift soon anyway." He kicked at his tire. "I'll ride first and take the lead," Hamish said and pulled away.

He was right about the fog. As they cycled by the last few houses it was already easier to see. The sun was a lemony haze in the sky as it burned away at the mist. The cars they passed had turned off their headlights.

"We're going off the road soon, get ready," Hamish yelled over his shoulder. There's a path just ahead to the right. Follow me."

The gravel on the shoulder crunched under their tires then they were off bumping along a path in the general direction of the sea. The fresh salty wind whistled against Annie's face and her hair blew free. It was wonderful to be out in it all again.

Ahead of them, past the Flying Club airstrip, stood

miles of open grassland where the local farmers let their sheep graze.

"The path ends soon. Watch out for rabbit holes," Hamish called again.

Kabooff!!! One of Annie's wheels dropped down into one. But experience brought her foot hard down on the pedal and she was quickly out with the bike under control.

The two wound their way across the rocky, bumpy grass in no particular direction that Annie could see.

"Do you know where you're going?" She yelled but the wind carried her voice away.

Suddenly she could see where the grass stopped and the cliff dropped down to the beach below. Hamish jumped off his bike and walked back.

"This is the first one. Does this seem about right?"

"We'll have to go closer to the edge to really see." She dropped her bike on the rough grass and they walked. She wanted to run but the on shore wind pushed too hard. There was a magnificent view from the top of the cliff and now that the fog had lifted they could see all the way out to the May Island.

"Oh look, Hamish! We were out there, *Bill* and I. It was wonderful."

The joy in her face made him smile. "So, is this where you left him?"

Annie scanned the sandy beach, the protective cove and the rocky headland but there was no sign of a sailboat. "No, I guess it isn't." She flopped down on the grass and hugged her knees.

"No problem," Hamish's voice was cheerful. "I know other places."

"Let's rest for a bit. You didn't bring anything to eat, did you?" She had been in far too big a rush to think of anything so practical.

"Just some peppermints." Hamish pulled a sticky package from his pocket. "Here, have one."

She picked one of the cleaner sweets from his hand. "Dear, Gran. She is a terrific lady you know," Annie said sucking on the peppermint. "I bet there aren't many grandmothers who'd do what she's doing."

"That's a fact. Your Mum wouldn't go round to check up, would she?"

"No time. Besides Gran told her we might go shopping together. Doesn't that take the cake?"

Hamish laughed and shook his head. "Amazing lady is right; but come on; we should get going." He stood up. "The sooner we get you back the better. The next place is a lot further."

*   *   *

Hamish wasn't kidding. The grassy fields stretched on for miles and got rockier and even more undermined by rabbit holes. The morning grew cool again, the pedaling harder. Finally he gave the word.

"It's over there, where the land rises," he dismounted. "We'll have to leave the bikes here."

"Can't we ride all the way up?"

"Not safe. Too steep; then there's a sudden drop, just at the last."

Annie looked where Hamish pointed. Those awful grey gun buildings stood on the rise. Dread seeped into her bones. There had been wrecks up and down this coast for hundreds of years. It made her evil dream more like the real version at every step.

"Please make this the wrong place," she prayed as they climbed.

*   *   *

But Annie may as well have 'saved her breath to cool her porridge' as grandfather McLeod used to say. When the two looked down on the cove below the sight that greeted them made her blood run cold.

"No!" Annie grabbed at Hamish's arm.

"Good grief, would you look at that!"

The few wisps of fog curling in the cove below were not enough to disguise the sight of a sailboat, tipped hard on its side, its mast snapped in two.

"It can't be; it can't," Anne fought back her tears.

She had never seen a full scale disaster like this. A broken model held none of the horror that this true life wreck presented. The beautiful hull had a huge gash, as though some giant had hammered a hole in its chest, allowing the sea to spill inside. The sails from the broken mast lay in blown out heaps like laundry scattered wildly from a hamper.

"I was responsible for this." Annie said her voice flat; her feelings numb.

"Don't be crazy."

"It's true."

"Annie, that's not *Bill* over there on the rocks, if that's what you mean. That's a real sailboat, wrecked and everything. And I bet it's not been there long either."

"What do you mean?"

"That storm, the night before last. Bet it happened then. We should go down there and take a look."

Annie gulped in deep breaths of salty air but it didn't lessen the pounding in her chest. "Just give me a minute, okay?"

But Hamish didn't wait. He whipped off his cap and stuffed it between his bicycle spokes then jumped and ran down the steep sand cliff, sure footed as a goat.

"Well," he stopped and turned, "are you coming or not?"

*   *   *

Annie stood at the top of the cliff. The beautiful *William Morr* was not going to be with her always, was he? Even though she'd rescued him once there was no way she could undo what she saw before her now. This was the real world where storms howl in, where ships are wrecked and people get sick and die no matter how much you love them.

"Annie! Come on!" Hamish waved his arms at her.

She wiped at the salty tears coursing down her cheeks. She sniffed till her nose stung. "All right, I'm coming!" She plunged down the hill after him.

*   *   *

Hamish had her hand when they waded into the chilly water. "It looks much bigger up close, doesn't it?" he said.

"Yeah, it does."

The yacht had come into the cove bow first and loomed above them. "It'll be hard getting up there onto the deck from here, Annie."

She stared up, her eyes still wet and prickling.

"Should we move round to the stern?" asked Hamish.

"No, I can see a line hanging over the starboard side. We can use that to shimmy up."

"You're right. I missed that."

Waves slapped against the broken hull and every so often the whole vessel shuddered.

Hamish stopped. "Are you sure it's safe to get on board?"

"Probably not very, but I'm going anyway," Annie dropped his hand and pushed ahead through the water.

"Maybe that's not such a good idea?"

"Hah, now who's a sissy?"

"Okay, okay, then you go first; you're lighter. We'll see how this holds." Hamish tugged on a line that flapped against the hull. "Seems okay. Try it slowly, but be careful!"

The line creaked as Annie ascended. It held just long enough for her to get a foothold on the deck, then it dropped away. "Phew! That was close!"

Hamish cupped his hand and called, "I'll go around to the stern and see if there's another line. Wait for me right where you are. Don't move. Okay?"

The water was deep enough to swim so Hamish struck out. When he reached the stern there were no lines to grab hold of but there was something far better; a ladder. He pulled on the rungs and hauled his soaking body out of the water and up to the broken stern rail. On the top step a heavy mat of seaweed blocked his way. He yanked it away then stared, open-mouthed. Huge letters, spelling out the name of the yacht, were painted across the stern. There was no way this could be right.

"Annie!" he yelled, but she couldn't hear him.

Chapter Eighteen

On Board

"Annie!" Hamish called again. "Over here!"

She moved across the sloping deck inching her way back towards the cockpit. The broken mast blocked her way. "Just a sec, I have to move to the other side." Annie pushed away mounds of canvas into the sea then grabbed at the lifelines for support. It took a while but she finally eased herself down into the cockpit, breathing heavily.

"Sit here a second, Annie," he pointed at the cockpit seats," I have to tell you something."

Annie didn't mind the rest. She shut her eyes and leaned back against the seat. "Shoot."

Hamish got up on his knees and leaned over the stern. "Right here; I saw it when I climbed up; the name of this boat."

"That's usually where they put it," her voice was flat.

"But Annie, you won't believe this. Come and read it for yourself. It says the *William Morr*!"

"Annie's eyes flew open. She stood up and leaned over beside Hamish and they pulled more of the weedy tangle aside. She could feel the raised letters under her fingers. Her hand shook as she traced the script. It was the proof she had been looking for.

"It is! We've found him. I told you we would!"

"But it can't be your *William Morr*, not your *Bill*, that's ridiculous!" Hamish ran his hands through his wind blown hair. "It's just some crazy coincidence."

"Or maybe not."

"Annie you really are nuts!"

They sat huddled together, shivering. Hamish was soaked through; Annie was wet to her waist.

"What are you gonna do now?"

"I'm going below." She stood up. "I need to know how bad it is down there too." She yanked at the drop board jammed sideways in the companionway.

"No, please. Don't go; it's not safe!" But she was already partway down.

*   *   *

The cabin was filled with an eerie light. Seaweed had draped itself over the portholes too and it took a moment for their eyes to adjust.

It was Annie who saw her first.

"Hamish, over there, on the bunk. Th-that's a p-person, isn't it?"

Hamish lunged at Annie trying to pull her back just as the boat shifted. The two of them tumbled onto the deck crashing up against a bank of lockers.

Annie screamed. So did Hamish.

The woman's mouth was open but her eyes weren't.

Annie shook. "Who is she? Is she…?"

"I don't know. Let's get out of here!" Hamish scrambled to his feet.

"Hey, where are you going?"

"I'm leaving. I'm not crazy about dead bodies."

"But we can't just leave her. Suppose she isn't dead? She may need help."

"All the more reason to go. We'll report it, Annie."

"You don't mean that! We have to help her and I have to find …"

"We've already found it," Hamish cut her off, "her!"

"No, please, this is the *William Morr*. I have to find out what this means; for Moira."

"Who the devil is Moira? Not her I hope?" He pointed at the woman.

An icy chill rippled through Annie's body. Coincidences; hideous coincidences. Annie slid onto the deck and stayed sitting there, her head in her hands.

"Annie, come *on*! We've got to get out of here. This can't have anything to do with you."

"But it might," her voice was a whisper.

Hamish stood over her, "Annie, this is not a game! We have to get help, real help!"

"I'm not playing a *game*; I need to know what really happened. There must be *something* here to explain it all."

"*This* is what happened, Annie, and she's a part of it." He flung his hand in the woman's direction.

"I can't believe you'd just leave."

"So, come with me, then."

A moan came from the direction of the prostrate woman.

"You see. She's not dead!" Annie scrambled to her feet. "Not yet anyway. Maybe I can save her."

"You! You don't know anything. You're not a doctor. You're not even a nurse." Hamish sounded as scared as she was.

"I took a first aid badge at Guides. I can keep her warm and comfortable at least."

There was a long pause then he turned to Annie. "*I* could do that; if you like."

She stared at him. "You would?"

"Yeah, I could stay instead. It really isn't safe for you here. You go. Go to the police. Tell *them* to come out and help."

"I couldn't, Hamish. Not the police; not again!" Annie voice was filled with dread.

"Oh come *on,* what else do you suggest, then?"

They sat together on the sloping deck, stunned by the whole discovery.

"Hold on a sec," said Hamish raising a finger, "I *did* just think of something."

"You did?" Her voice rose with hope. "Tell me."

"The radio; every boat has a radio; for emergencies or for calling ahead to see if it's okay to bring your boat in safely; if you don't know the harbour; that sort of thing."

"You're right. A woman I just read about; the one who sailed round the world alone; Naomi something or other; she called her radio her 'lifeline'."

"Then let's find it," Hamish said, some of his lost confidence returning.

It wasn't hard; it was mounted on the bulkhead right above the chart table. Hamish unclipped the microphone and pushed the button on the side. "Craig harbour rescue… Craig harbour rescue this is the yacht *William Morr…* come in please."

"Impressive, Hamish. Have you done this before?" Annie smiled.

"It's just correct voice procedure. I know stuff like that."

"Still."

"Craig harbour rescue… Craig harbour rescue this is the yacht *William Morr…* come in please. This is an emergency." Hamish repeated, louder this time, and waited.

They both waited but nothing came back except crackling noises.

"Third time lucky?" He looked at Annie then, holding down the button on the microphone he spoke again. Still nothing but static.

"I think it's shorted out; the sea water must have messed up the wires. Damn; I really thought this would work."

"Me too. So we're back to *going* for help. But, Hamish, the police are a bad idea; it has to be someone with a boat."

"Another boat! You can't mean it!"

Annie's mind was spinning. Who could help, quickly? Someone she could trust not to bring in the police, at least not until she got home; until Gran was off the hook. Was she using Gran as an excuse? Still, the thought of the police and all she'd gone through just two days ago made her feel weak in the knees.

"Can you think a little faster, Annie? I really don't like hanging around here."

"I don't like it either. But I'm in a real jam here 'cause of all the other stuff that's happened. The police scare me to bits."

"You should be thinking about that poor woman before yourself, Annie."

"I *am*! I'm volunteering to stay with her, aren't I?"

"Look, Annie, no fighting, okay. Things are bad enough."

Annie leaned back and rubbed at her bruised knee. More minutes passed in silence before she said, "I might have an idea."

"Get on with it, then, please!"

"Do you know Tam Dewart?"

"Who?"

"Tam *Dewart*. He's Molly's husband. You know the Molly who works for my Mum at the hotel?"

"Don't know the name."

"Yes, you do. He's a fisherman, *and*, most important, he has a small boat. My Dad's been out with him a couple of times."

"Oh, a shrimpy little guy; curly hair kind of; a pipe in his mouth all the time."

"That's the one."

"So you could pick him out?"

"Maybe."

"Then go find him and get him to come out here with his boat. It's the only way."

"Geez, Annie, this is even crazier than all your other ideas."

"No it isn't, because it has to be a boat. We'd never get her up that cliff. And there's no road up there either."

"You're blotto. You want to take this woman all the way back in a fishing boat?"

She ignored him. "Listen. Molly says he spends a lot of time at the *'Gull and Spoon'*. I bet if you went there you'd find him or someone who could tell you where he is."

"That's a pub. Kid's aren't allowed in."

"That shouldn't bother you. Anyway, we haven't much choice. Will you do it?"

There was a long silence then Hamish shook his head.

"No, Annie. If we want to save this woman we'll have to do it a whole lot faster than Tam ever could."

She was ready to give in. "Okay, you're right. The whole thing's going to blow up in our faces anyway."

"So you'll go? To the police now? And *I'll* stay?" Hamish tried to end the discussion and move on.

"No, *I'll* stay and you go; but to the *Coast Guard*, not the police. Maybe Daddy's off duty today. Maybe we can fix this without my parents knowing."

"Fat chance."

"Yeah, well…"

Hamish made no move to leave. "Oh brother. It's really not safe here and I could be ages."

"Stop fussing; besides I need time. Maybe I'll find some answers while you're gone."

"Answers? Right you do that." He noted Annie's frown and changed tack, "Your parents are going to kill me, you know."

"They'll kill me too," Annie grinned, "We'll die together."

Hamish raked his fingers through the ruffled mess of his hair.

"Anyway what choice do we have?" She braced herself against the angled bunk, "Someone has to stay with her."

"O...k...a...y," Hamish sighed. "But you will be careful? Promise? *Really* careful. Don't move around too much."

"I'll be really careful, Hamish."

"I'm off then," he squeezed her shoulder and stood up, "and I'll be back as fast as I can."

* * *

At the Coast Guard office that morning Malcolm Brodie, Sandy McLeod's second in command, received an urgent phone call.

"This is Adam Wakefield speaking; of Wakefield Yachts in Glasgow."

"Yes, Mr. Wakefield."

"I want to report an overdue vessel; name's *The Morr*. Have you by any chance had a distress call from her?"

"Can't say for certain, sir. There was a message came in late the night before last, during the storm, but it was badly garbled. It cut out before any identification or position could be given."

"And you didn't send out the cutter?"

"Yes we did, actually. The lads made it some distance up the coast before they were forced to turn back but they didn't see anything. The coastline is treacherous. It's full of inlets and rocks and in high seas they couldn't move in for a closer look without endangering their own vessel. But I don't need to explain that to you, sir."

"And yesterday?" Wakefield broke in.

"Very high winds; then fog; crazy weather. Never seen anything like it. Lads still had to keep well away from the coastline. They didn't see anything then either and the fog again this morning. But we've been out a couple of times anyway. As I'm sure you know, when the visibility is bad like this we rely pretty heavily on responses to our foghorn blasts."

"And you heard nothing?"

"Nothing at all, sir."

"Can you send a cutter out now?"

"I would sir but it's on another search at the moment. The lads've been working round the clock since the storm. As soon as it gets back I'll brief the new crew and tell them to try again.

There was a pause on the line before Wakefield came back. "I will leave you my telephone number here in Glasgow and at my home in Glen Fellan. Please contact me as soon as you hear anything. It's my daughter Katherine who's on board. She was skippering the boat alone."

"We certainly will, sir." Malcolm wrote down the contact numbers along with Wakefield's name and placed them in the file tray on his desk.

Chapter Nineteen

Who is She?

Annie sat with her knees drawn up on the bare boards of the deck. She was studying the woman's face. She had managed to prop her up into a sort of sitting position so that her legs weren't so twisted as before. They had looked awful up close lying all at a weird angle. There was some caked blood on her trousers too. Annie touched the nearer leg ever so lightly and thought she felt the sharpness of a broken bone.

But the woman was definitely breathing. Annie could see her chest move up and down. Periodically her eyelids would flicker. Her mouth stayed pretty well open. Not wide, just enough to make breathing easier. She'd done that herself when she had a bad cold.

There were some blankets in one of the locker drawers. She threw one over the woman's chest and tucked it around her neck. Another she arranged very gently over her injured legs then took away the empty water bottles lying next to her.

She stuffed a cushion behind her head. That was the warm and comfortable part, but what else might she need to do to keep this person alive? Anything else was pretty much beyond her.

She could try talking to her. The silence between them was giving her the creeps.

"My name's Annie," she began. "I'm twelve years old; almost thirteen actually. I live in a big stone house overlooking the sea not far from here. I have a cat called Bozz but he disappeared a few nights ago when I was out looking for…" she stopped.

It felt dumb talking out loud. If she had something to read, it would be much better. A book, even a dull one, would pass the time. She thought of all the books she had at home, her favorite adventures, mysteries and folk tales, the fabulous pictures she had spent hours dreaming over and climbing into.

"Do you like to read?" Annie studied the woman's face again. She looked young for a woman; a lot younger than her mother and it surprised her that the straggling blonde hair that had escaped from her pony tail did nothing to spoil her pretty face.

"Do you like mysteries?"

Annie glanced round the tumbled cabin looking for the familiar sight of book spines. Above the chart table was a small collection. She eased her way over and picked up a title or two. Cruising Guide: East Neuk of Fife was mostly charts. North Atlantic Crossings was a thicker book with small print and very scary pictures. She was about to pick it up anyway when another caught her eye: <u>First Aid at Sea!</u>

This was perfect; exactly what she needed. She turned the pages, squinting in the poor light and began to read aloud: *"The unconscious casualty... There are numerous causes of unconsciousness, head injury, shock, poisoning...* Not the last I don't think."

Her eyes scanned the page looking for something helpful. *"The first aider must proceed as follows: ensure that the air passages are not obstructed. Remove false teeth,"* Annie giggled. *"Clear the mouth of mucous, blood, vomit...* oh, yuk!" She took a closer look at the woman's face. Her mouth was still open and she was breathing, thank heavens.

"Loosen the clothing about neck, chest and waist..." She looked again. It was amazing what she hadn't noticed. The life jacket clipped around her chest had ridden up higher than it should. The straps looked stretched. If she undid the clasp it would make her more comfortable.

Over the next hour or so Annie worked around her patient, referring to the first aid book and noting the importance of keeping any broken bones well supported. The horror of the situation lessened with each task. She checked for injuries other than the obvious ones to her legs. She noted there were bruises on her lower arms and a few cuts on her hands. They had dried blood on them but did not look infected.

She could try taking her pulse next. She placed two fingers against the woman's neck where her Guide leader had told them to. She could feel a faint sensation in her fingers. Was this a good pulse? Then she had the brain wave to take her own and compare them. Hers was really banging away, probably because she was pretty upset.

The woman's eyes flickered again. She sighed and moved her head ever so slightly.

* * *

Annie had been unprepared for the woman waking up. She flipped through the book again, hands trembling and found something: *"As consciousness returns to the casualty speak reassuringly. Moisten the casualty's lips with water and gently restrain him or her to prevent further injury."*

That would be fresh water, obviously. Annie got up slowly from the tilted deck and tried the tap in the galley sink. It made a hissing sound then a gurgle. Nothing came out; not one drop. The tap in the tiny bathroom was the same.

She began opening doors and pulling stuff out onto the floor of the cabin, cans of fish, baked beans, biscuits, canned peaches, and from another locker bars of soap, steel wool, paint thinner.

All the searching and pulling things about made the cabin look even more of a disaster zone. Then she tried a locker far up in the bow and hauled out a collection of lines. No water containers; only lines. Some were in a real mess; one was even tangled around fish netting as well.

"This is hopeless!" She heaved the whole knotted mess onto the deck. Then she heard a clunk. A water bottle? No such luck, just a chunk of driftwood caught inside. As she reached to push it away she saw something she had missed. This piece of "driftwood" was shiny and an unmistakable shape. She closed her eyes then opened them again very slowly and gaped at the object sticking out of the lines and netting. Could it be *Bill*? She rubbed her eyes and looked again. But no; it was nothing more than some stupid piece of wooden flotsam; a shiny chunk, but not the *William Morr* by a long shot.

Chapter Twenty

On the Edge

Hamish's bicycle bumped down the cobbled street toward the harbour where the ancient stone buildings crowded in on one another. There were fishermen's houses, tackle shops, shops that sold postcards and souvenirs and a pub with its sign swinging out over the street showing an old grey gull with a gold spoon in its beak.

He passed all these and headed for the coast guard station. It sat on a rise above the harbour with a full view of the inlet. But when he reached the station there was no one in sight. He looked down to the harbour but saw no sign of the cutter either. The only boats tied up there belonged to fishermen and were hardly suitable for the rescue he had in mind. He shaded his eyes from the sun and looked everywhere.

"What are ye after, laddie?" asked a passing fisherman.

"The Coast Guard cutter; is it here somewhere? I'd ask at the station but no one's there."

"Cutter's awa' on a rescue. You'll not be finding any-one laddie; not for a time anyway. The police launch too, it's out. Bad times, laddie, bad times with that storm and all."

The man might have chatted on all afternoon had Hamish been willing. He excused himself and with a heavy heart set out to put Annie's backup plan into action.

Hamish was shivering now but not from cold. The ride had warmed him up and mostly dried his wet cloth-ing. It must be nerves, he thought.

It was past lunchtime but the 'Gull and Spoon' was still jammed with wool jerseyed and booted fisherman. There was a distinctly fishy odor mixed in with a sour fug that Hamish realized was beer. He stood up taller, trying to look older and pulled his cap lower over his face. The smoky air dulled the lighting and provided extra cover. The gray haze settled most heavily over the bar where the spigots were arranged in rows.

"What'll ye have, Jock?" bellowed the barman, "the usual?"

"Aye; and no skimping on it now, will ye?"

There was much shoving and pushing as Hamish worked his way past the bar. The men, desperate to quench their thirst, were none too polite about it.

"Hey, that was my foot!" Hamish squawked, for-getting to keep this mouth shut. His voice still hadn't deepened. It was a dead give-away.

"And what's this young lad doing here?" scoffed one of the heftier patrons. "Is it a pint you're after?" Hoots of laughter burst around him.

"No, no. I'm looking for Tam Dewart."

"Tam is it? Anyone hear o' that name?" The loud tone was mocking. Hamish squirmed and tried to move away but the big man blocked him. "Now laddie, you better move out. If Dugald sees ye, he'll no mind tossing ye in the dustbin wi' the fish guts."

"No, please. I really need to speak to Tam Dewart."

"Och, Rory, leave the lad alone." A smallish man in the waterproof leggings and rubber boots came towards them.

"I'm just trying to teach this scamp a lesson. He knows he canna come in here. Bold as brass he is."

The small fisherman ignored Rory's bluster. "Is it Tam Dewart ye're after?"

"Yes. Are you Tam Dewart, sir?"

"Och, no; I'm Alec, his brother. What would you be wanting wi' him that could'na wait?"

"I, I need to speak to him. But I really should ask him myself."

"Come wi' me, then; no need ta worry about Dugald or Rory."

The men had lost interest in Hamish by now so he and Alec found their way easily to a table by the window. A man looking much like Alec sat next to its smudgy glass.

"Tam, there's someone here wants a word wi' ye."

Frowning, Alec's brother looked up from his suds.

"And who would you be, lad?"

"Hamish Findlay, sir."

"I'll leave you two then." Alec moved away.

*   *   *

"I'm a friend of Annie's, sir, Annie MacLeod." Hamish eased into a chair opposite Tam. "You know her, don't you?"

His frown vanished. "O' course I do. My Molly works for the missus."

"Yes, well, Annie," Hamish coughed nervously, "she needs your help, sir. There's been some trouble you see."

"Trouble? What sort of trouble?"

"She, um, well she…" Hamish looked around uneasily.

"Out with it lad, though why you're asking me and not Mr. MacLeod I canna' guess."

"You have a boat, sir, and Annie's dad; he's already out with the cutter."

But he couldn't finish because Rory was striding toward them with the barman in tow. The scowl on Dugald's face revealed a set of stained and crooked teeth.

Tam waved him off. "It's alright, we're leaving. No need for a big fuss." Tam stood, a bit unsteadily, and pushed Hamish ahead of him out a side door.

*   *   *

They found a sunny piece of harbour wall to sit on and Hamish launched into his tale but left out the part about the woman. She could even be dead by now for all he knew.

"And just as we were leaving the boat," he went on, "Annie called down to me that there was something else on board she wanted to look for. She said she'd only be a minute."

"Ye should no' have climbed on board at all. Once

a boat's on the rocks anything can happen wi' her,"
scolded Tam. He took out a pipe from his pocket and
stuffed something brown and stringy into it.

"I know that now. But we just wanted to see. When
we got there it looked safe," Hamish lied. "Anyway, I
thought Annie was right behind me when I left so I let
myself down onto the rocks and waited. Then the boat
shifted; a lot. So we really need to get back there fast,
Mr. Dewart."

"Could you no' get back up to help her?" Tam took
a long drag from his smoldering pipe.

"Not the way the boat was then. Besides she was
shouting for me to get someone stronger. I think she
said something had fallen and jammed. She didn't
think I could get her out by myself."

"And what were ye twa doing there in the first place?"

Hamish found himself inventing on the fly, adding
to his story any way he could to make the man agree.
"Annie was upset about losing her cat," he paused.
"We've been everywhere looking for him." This was
taking too long. Hamish wiped a bead of sweat from
his forehead.

"You didn'a think it'd walked all the way out tae
the cove, surely?"

"Well, I didn't, but Annie did. She told me some story
about Bozz following her to the beach the other night
and she thought the cat might still be after her…" then
he trailed off swearing silently for this careless remark.

"Aye, it's true, a cat will wander," Tam said, not
picking up on the finer details. "Poor wee Annie. She's
that soft-hearted."

"So I agreed to go looking with her," Hamish

rushed on, "and that's when we found the wreck. Can we go now? Please, Mr. Dewart?"

"Her Da will have more than a cat fit when he finds out where she is."

"Maybe we won't need to tell him," Hamish said, not believing it for a minute. His stories were very muddled in his own head now. He had mixed the truth in with so many falsehoods.

*   *   *

Tam emptied his pipe against the wall and walked nimbly down the sloping cobbled breakwater with Hamish in pursuit.

"Ye ken, it's still no' a verra good time o' day for me lad," he said, shaking his head and slowing his pace. "My nets need work and my boat too afore the afternoon gets on. Molly has my tea on at five. I've no wish to rile her."

Hamish prayed he wasn't about to change his mind. "Annie's really counting on you, sir. She might even be hurt. Please, Mr. Dewart, we should hurry."

Tam stopped and scratched at his unshaven face. "Ach weel, then," he let out a long sigh, "I canna' leave Annie like that. Molly will just hafta wait."

Hamish breathed normally again. Tam would do it.

*   *   *

When they reached the wall where Tam's boat was tied Hamish stared down in dismay. The tide was low. It was a long way down the seaweed-covered ladder and the boat secured alongside looked very small.

"You go out in that!"

"I do indeed, laddie. She's a fine wee gurl." Tam started down the ladder, "It's many years we've had thegither. You can trust my *Molly Girl* in any sea." He was on board now pulling a cover off the outboard engine.

"Yes, uh, I was just expecting something a bit, you know, bigger, that's all." Hamish looked over his shoulder and placed his foot on the first slippery rung.

"Bigger! What good is that? You need water tight, nimble and when needs be, fast." Tam looked up, his voice was sharp.

Then why was it, Hamish wondered as he stepped on board, that there were several inches of water sloshing around? He shoved aside a couple of lobster pots to make room to sit then rested his shoes against the drier sides of the boat.

Tam leaned to the stern of *Molly Girl* and tinkered with the motor. It didn't start. He adjusted the throttle and tried again. The engine coughed.

"You'll be needing to replace that one!" called a fellow fisherman. Hamish gripped his seat and waited. He kept his arms well inboard away from the tangle of lines and metal hooks. The motor caught.

"Mr. Dewart," Hamish asked above the chugging, "are you leaving *all* these pots in the boat? It seems very crowded, don't you think?"

"Och, no, there's plenty of room for Annie beside me."

"Right, of course there is." Hamish squirmed. But the body? Where would it go?

"Then we'll be off. Tie that line up yonder on the ladder. We'll be needing it when we get back."

Chapter Twenty-One

Katherine

It may have been a couple of hours before the woman opened her eyes. Annie didn't see when it happened because she had dozed off herself.

"Hello, Annie?" said the woman, her voice thick.

"Oh!" Annie jumped. "Did I wake you?"

The woman coughed. "No... been listening; for a while."

"I thought I was just talking to myself." Annie made herself smile; reassuringly she hoped.

"I heard you. It's Annie, isn't it?"

"Yes."

"I'm Katherine," the woman struggled to speak. "I thought that...that maybe I dreamt you?"

"I'm not a dream," Annie reassured her, though she felt the whole scene in the wrecked cabin was more dreamlike than real.

The woman reached out and touched Annie's arm her eyes wide and staring. "Yes," she sighed, "real..."

"Yes."

"So afraid no one would…that I might…"

"Don't say it, please."

"But someone older *is* coming?"

"Yes, of course. We haven't much longer to wait, I'm sure," Annie said feeling anything but sure. "Everything will be alright."

"Alright, yes, you are here… now." She shut her eyes again.

Annie had never been much at talking to grownups she didn't know but she dreaded the silence again now that Katherine had spoken. "I've been reading this." She held up the copy of <u>First Aid at Sea.</u> "I've been learning how to help."

The woman let her chin drop; a tiny nod.

"I hope I'm doing the right thing," Annie continued brightly.

"You are…thank you," She tugged at the blankets then winced.

Annie leaned closer. "Are you hurting? What can I do?"

"Some water, please… I'm very thirsty."

"Oh, dear. I've looked everywhere. The taps don't seem to work."

Katherine hesitated, her brow furrowed. A shaky arm pointed across the cabin. "…under that bunk…lift the cushion; there's a lid…"

Annie moved carefully over the uneven deck. There were several large jugs of water stacked under the berth. She poured some into a plastic tumbler, dipped her fingers into the water and wiped the woman's lips. She had never touched a stranger in such a personal way before.

"That's good, Annie, so good." Katherine slumped back against the cushion. Her eyes closed again.

* * *

The little fishing boat rolled out from the calm harbour waters into an easterly swell. The water was just an arm's length from the boat rail. The air was cool in spite of the sun. Hamish started shivering again.

"I've an oilskin, here, laddie." Tam extracted a smelly yellow bundle from a pocket at the side of the boat. Hamish slipped it on.

Hamish hadn't seen the harbour from the sea side before. He turned around as much as he dared. The gunnels were awfully close to the water.

"How far out do you drop your pots?" Hamish yelled.

"Over yonder." He pointed toward an island. Tam wasn't much of a talker. It was hard to hear anyway in the wind with the motor running and the constant wash of the surf along the hull.

"How deep is it out here?"

"Five to six fathoms, depending."

Hamish did a quick calculation. A fathom was about six feet. They could be skimming over forty feet of frigid ocean! He pulled the oilskin closer.

Hamish cupped his hands and shouted. "How soon till we get there?"

Tam shrugged, "Depends."

It had to be over two hours since he'd left Smuggler's Cove. How would Annie be holding up? And that woman? He shivered again. The smelly oilskin was making him nauseous.

"This must be faster than by land, right?"

"Yup."

"There're lots of rocks in close," Hamish explained.

"I know the place."

They purred on, the swell increasing with the wind. Hamish could feel his stomach heaving.

Tam grinned. "Put your head over the side if you feel the need."

"Thanks." In an agonized gush he lost the scant contents of his stomach overboard.

"That should do it, lad."

And it did; for a little while.

*   *   *

The hulk of the boat shifted again and water began to trickle through the murky portholes like a bath tap that wouldn't shut off. It landed on the padded cushions of the berth with a thrumming sound.

Annie dragged another blanket and stuffed it around the opening. It made the cabin darker but the dripping stopped.

"That's better." Annie tried to sound cheerful.

"Is...is...there another b...blanket?" Katherine's teeth chattered then her whole body began to tremble.

"I used the last dry one on the porthole. I'm so sorry. Now they're all soaking."

"Annie, it's okay." Katherine paused then spoke barely above a whisper, "We'll ...we'll try something else."

*   *   *

The small coal oil lamp responded to the match and glowed with a warm light. Annie lifted it down from the bracket and set it on the deck beside them. The gentle heat it gave off stopped Katherine from shivering though her face was flushed with fever. Then her lips moved and she tried to speak again.

"The wind…started to pick up…" Katherine said forcing the words out.

"Hush now," Annie soothed, afraid the effort would be too much.

"…some fish net in the water…I couldn't risk…" her breathe came in gasps. "…it would catch in the propeller…"

"Try a little of this," Annie held the glass to Katherine's lips. She was terrified Katherine might pass out, or worse, if she spoke too long but at the same time she was mesmerized by her words. It was as if Katherine had slid right into her nightmare. Or had she, Annie, slipped into hers?

Katherine sipped for a second or two then pushed the glass away. "… too dangerous if the engine failed… had to pull it on…on… the deck." Perspiration beaded on her forehead.

"You threw it in the anchor locker, didn't you?" Annie said, a bit ashamed of her eager question.

"Yes...but how…?"

"I was looking for water up there. I found the netting and…" she couldn't finish.

"Annie?"

"It's nothing. Sorry, I'm okay," she struggled to keep her voice steady. "It's just that I was looking for something."

"Looking…for…?"

It was *Bill* of course; but it made no sense.

"You found it? Annie?" Katherine persisted despite the effort it caused.

"No. I thought I had but…"Annie broke off. She mustn't alarm Katherine.

Katherine's face drained of colour. "…the cove… the sea wild and the rocks so close…not ready for the hit…"

"Please; try to rest now." Annie stroked the woman's hand then leaned back and shut her own eyes for a moment so that she did not see the little rivers of water snaking across the deck. The blanket had fallen away from the porthole. The boat was being dragged by the rising tide across the rocks and farther into the sea.

Chapter Twenty-Two

Unravelling

Margaret McLeod was having a very busy day. Four new visitors, all elderly ladies, had arrived a day earlier than expected and their rooms had to be prepared. Aileen was out of sorts, scrambling with fresh linens and couldn't help Molly in the dining room at lunch. And there had been a mix up with the butcher's delivery which meant a last minute change to the dinner menu.

"Could you contact Tam and ask him to get us something, Molly? Whatever he has from the morning catch would be fine. Mackerel; sole; anything."

"I'll send the delivery lad with a message," Molly offered. "It'll be Ewan today. He won't mind. He'll be here within the hour. He can stop by the pub where Tam takes his lunch and bring something round in the afternoon."

"Oh, thank you Molly," Margaret sighed with relief. "You're a wonder!"

*   *   *

But when Ewan came to the kitchen door that afternoon he had a parcel from the butcher shop under his arm.

Molly was brusque, "And where's the fish I asked you to get from Tam?"

"Who is it, Molly?" called Margaret McLeod, anxious to have the evening's dinner settled.

Ewan brought his fingers to his lips.

"It's someone to see me madam. I won't be a moment," Molly pulled the door behind her and stepped outside.

"What's going on, Ewan? Where's the fish?"

"It's about Tam. He'd gone off in his boat wi' a young lad by the time I got to 'The Gull' so I brought you some chops from McGarry's instead." Ewan gave the parcel to Molly. "That's what Alec told me. Said there was some trouble or other and the lad wanted Tam to help."

"What lad? What sort o' trouble?"

"It might've been the Findlay boy that was askin' after Tam. Dugald thought that's who had the cheek to come right inta the 'Gull'.

"You mean, Hamish, Annie's friend?"

"If that's his name."

Molly's face crumpled.

"Alec thought he *might* have overheard Annie's name mentioned at that," Ewan added.

"Annie? No. Madam told me she's with her Gran today."

"Oh, I see. Well then, maybe I'm mistaken. But it's strange. Tam going out in the afternoon 'n' all."

"It is that. And if it was with Hamish something's more than fishy."

*   *   *

Molly leaned against the door frame for a few minutes and watched Ewan pedal off on his bicycle. It was almost time for her to slip home and fix Tam's tea anyway so she could easily stop by Mrs. Robertson's on the way. No sense in worrying Madam when she's already up to her ears. It was probably just some silly misunderstanding. Molly slipped back inside and pulled off her apron.

"I'll be back in an hour, Madam. Ewan's delivery is in the refrigerator," Molly called in a cheery voice.

"That fine, Molly. Aileen and I can manage till then. Say hello to Tam."

I hope I can do that, Molly thought, swinging herself up on her bicycle.

*   *   *

Gran kept looking at the clock. What was keeping Annie? She and Hamish should have been finished their explorations by now. Margaret was unlikely to phone, much less drop by, still, Gran's discomfort was becoming acute.

"I should *never* have agreed to this. And with Hamish to boot," she fussed aloud. It was going to be trouble again.

By three o'clock Gran was in such a state that the

knock at her door made her heart pop like an overfilled balloon.

"Annie!" she burst out, opening the door.

"Mrs. Robertson. No, it's me, Molly."

"And it is too!"

"You're no' expecting Annie, are you? She's here already is she no'?" Molly felt flustered and sure she was saying the wrong things.

"Yes. Well no, she's stepped out for a wee while. She's off to pick up a few things from the grocer's," Gran lied.

"Oh, that's good. I was that worried since Ewan dropped by. There's been some strange business to-day. But if Annie is hereabouts after all then I'll be getting on."

"No, wait Molly. Come away in, please. I'd like to have a word."

*   *   *

"It's over there I think, Mr. Dewart, just around those rocks."

"Aye, laddie, I see. And by the looks of her we may be only just in time.

The boat was tipped almost completely over on her side the sea lapping against the half submerged portholes.

Tam slowed the motor. "This'll tak some doing Hamish. I need to tie *Molly Girl* here but we canna risk a line around yon boat." Tam scanned the cove looking for a safe place to attach a line.

"Ach, that may do," he pointed to an old mooring

to their starboard. "Tak this line. Can ye get it through there?"

"Shouldn't we try for one closer to the yacht?"

"Even if there was one," Tam looked cross at needing to explain, "I dinna want to be close to her if she moves."

Hamish leaned, struggling to feed the line through the rusted loop atop the float. "I think that's got it."

"All right, bring the rest of it back here."

For a first time sailor, Hamish moved pretty fast.

Tam tested the line. "Good, that should hold. Now, where did you and Annie get aboard?"

"We climbed up on the far side of the deck sir, but it was a lot higher then. It should be easier now, shouldn't it?"

"But verra dangerous. It'll no tak *my* weight. Ye'll have to get aboard on your own and see what needs to be moved; see where we can get her out."

The low tide that had made the wreck easy to reach before was higher now. It would mean another swim to get there. Hamish was getting used to being soaked for Annie's sake.

Tam uncoiled another fishy line and tied it around Hamish's waist. "Ye'll no drift too far in the current with this. Now; any trouble, give it a pull and I'll know where ye are."

To this line Tam added another. "When ye get tae Annie, tie this round her. Then I'll ha'e ye both. All right now, laddie, jump!"

Hamish hesitated. Should he tell Tam about the other woman now? Would it change anything? Lord, this was a mess.

"Not yet, wait. There's something I…"

"Laddie, this is no time fer cold feet. I'm right out o' patience. I shouldn'a be here in the first place. Now for the love of heaven let's get Annie and go home afore I change my mind and fetch the police."

Hamish had no choice. He jumped with a heavy splash and stroked out for the rocks the line paying out behind him.

Tam watched the dripping boy scale the rocks and disappear on the far side of the wreck. He tugged on the line. He felt Hamish tug back. But after he moved behind the sailboat the line snagged so that tugging on it made no difference.

"Laddie, make haste!" Tam was close to jumping overboard himself.

* * *

The stern ladder was at such a wicked angle now Hamish had to get aboard by snagging the remaining stump of the mast and hauling himself up that way. He crawled, almost in tears from exhaustion and worry, toward the cockpit and peered through the open hatch into the cabin. He was unprepared for the sight that greeted him there. The woman was sitting almost up-right squashed against a berth that was tilted wickedly off side. The deck had become the sloping wall of the cabin.

"Annie!" Hamish yelled making Annie knock the lantern. The cabin went black.

* * *

"Can you see me?" he called into the shadows."

"We're over here," Annie waved. "Is… is Daddy with you?"

"No, the cutter was out; the whole crew with it; but Tam's here."

"Tam, really?" Annie now realized what a mad idea this had been. "Will there be room?"

"I don't know; Tam doesn't know about her." Hamish pointed to Katherine. "He thinks he's just come for you."

"You didn't tell him?"

"I was afraid he wouldn't come if he knew."

"Right; maybe that was best. So, what do we do now?"

"Get you both out; somehow." Hamish's eyes, adjusted to the gloom, took in the scene. "This place is a mess!"

"This boat is sinking, Hamish, in case you've forgotten!"

"Sorry; give me a minute. It's been a crazy afternoon, you know."

"Mine too; you were gone forever."

"I know. Look, we can do this, Annie, okay?" He touched her arm.

She nodded.

"Okay; good. Now first, we're going to need something to lay her on."

"You're right. I hadn't thought that far."

"Annie?" It was Katherine's breathy voice. "The door… to the forward cabin… just a couple of screws... get it off."

"Here, let me," Hamish crawled by the two of them.

Then he raised his leg and kicked out with his heel. The frame splintered leaving the door hanging by a single twisted hinge. He yanked it off.

"Holy cow! That was fast."

He said nothing just whipped one of the lines from his waist and pulled the door alongside Katherine while Annie eased her onto her back.

"Careful, Hamish; her legs; I think they're broken."

"I'll try not to touch them. If we lay the door long ways we can support her legs and her body too."

He spoke to Katherine. "Can you roll onto your side?"

Little by little they worked the cabin door under one side of Katherine's body then covered her with blankets.

"There that's one." Hamish's voice was calm now. "Now, can you try that again? Turn the other way?"

A sharp cry escaped Katherine's lips. They froze. One leg had swung free of the door. Hamish gritted his teeth and gently eased the leg back in place.

"Nearly there. Just a moment more," Annie soothed, "and we'll have you all wrapped up."

They passed the line under the door and all around her too securing her firmly in place.

"All set, then?" Hamish asked.

But the human parcel that was Katherine had fainted.

*   *   *

The light was changing as the sun moved lower and disappeared behind the protective cliffs of the cove. The tide continued to rise till, all at once, the wreck moved massively onto its side.

"Hamish!" yelled Tam, "For the love of heaven, hurry!"

*   *   *

As the yacht fell, seawater began filling up the cabin. The water rose round them taking with it any loose thing that would float: lifejackets, cushions and the parcel that was Katherine.

"Quick!" Annie shouted, grabbing a couple of jackets and holding them under the door for buoyancy, "push her out the hatch, NOW!"

"Holee!" yelled Hamish, "and I thought we were all goners!"

Annie had the most insane desire to laugh. It was so wild and so unspeakably lucky, their three bodies floating together into the cockpit and past the stern rail. She looked back for a second and saw the letters -M-O-R-R- disappear sideways into the sea. As soon as they were clear of the wreck Hamish tugged at the line that led back to Tam. He raised his arm and signaled. Tam waved back.

*   *   *

Tam saw the two swimmers emerging from the stern of the wreck. One was Hamish right enough, and the other Annie, thank heaven. But what was that large floating object they were pulling alongside them? Tam blinked and rubbed his eyes. Good lord, he thought, it looked for all the world like a body; a body tied to a plank and moving toward him.

Chapter Twenty-Three

What!

It was late afternoon when Margaret McLeod glanced out the kitchen window and saw Gran and Molly coming up the walk. "What's going on, Molly?" she demanded flinging open the door. "And *Mother*? Where's Annie? She's not with you?"

Molly just stood on the step. Gran walked right in. "Margaret, I'm afraid you are going to be *verry* angry with me."

"Come sit down, Mother, before you fall down." She guided her into a chair next to the kitchen table. "You look awful."

"And I feel awful too," Gran said untying the scarf from her hair.

"I really don't have time for this today, mother, so please tell me quickly, whatever it is."

Gran shrank back into her chair. "Hold on, Margaret, let me catch my breath."

"I'm getting more upset by the second. Is Annie all right? At least tell me that."

"I'm not sure, Margaret." Gran said after a moment. "You see I have allowed your very persuasive daughter to go off adventuring again."

"You did what?" Margaret McLeod almost shouted.

Gran crumpled the scarf in her hands. "Annie came to see me yesterday as you may know. What you don't know is that during her visit she… well she talked me into something I wish she hadn't."

"I don't believe it! Why would you let her take you in that way?"

"Stop, Margaret. Let me finish; please. Annie and Hamish planned to cycle out to one of the coves up the coast. She was desperate to find something."

"She and *Hamish*! Mother, how *could* you?"

"She was so determined, Margaret, and she knew you would never agree."

"Of course I wouldn't! Did she tell you what happened the other night?" She didn't wait for an answer. She sat right next to her mother and glared. "She could have drowned! How could you do this?"

Gran pulled away.

"I'll put on the kettle for some tea," Molly whispered.

"And you're in on this too, Molly?"

"Not really, madam. I…it was…"

Margaret McLeod threw up her hands. "I don't believe it! First my own mother, and now you Molly and neither of you with the foggiest idea where Annie is!"

Molly clutched the tea caddy in both hands, "I know a little about it, Madam. You see, when Ewan came by he was asking after Annie."

"Ewan was?"

Molly set the caddy down, removed the lid, and spooned tea leaves into the pot, "It worried me like, but you were so busy madam I hated to disturb you. So I went to see Mrs. Robertson, on my way home, thinking to make sure Annie was there, after all. But I wasn't really going home because I knew Tam was out fishing. That is, I thought he was."

"Molly, you're not making any sense!"

"Margaret, we think that if Hamish is with Tam there is a very good chance that Annie is too," Gran said, her scarf in a knot now.

"But why?" Margaret stood up.

"I can only think that they needed help and were too frightened to ask you, or Sandy, or the police."

"Well I have no such trouble, Mother, I'm calling them both!"

*   *   *

A scene was developing at the harbour. As soon as Sandy McLeod received the phone call from his wife he headed out in the Coast Guard cutter along with Malcolm. They sighted Tam's overloaded dory about a mile off the harbour entrance and pulled alongside.

"Annie; Hamish; what in God's name do you think you are doing! Your mother, Gran and I have been frantic!!"

Annie shrank from the anger in her father's voice. "Hello, Daddy," she gave a weak smile. She briefly waved one hand then quickly returned it alongside the other to steady the door balanced crossways on

Molly Girl's gunnels. Hamish held on tighter than ever with his two.

"And what the devil is that you have on board, Tam?" Sandy shielded his eyes against the lowering sun. He squinted at the bundle lashed to the cabin door. "What do you make of this, Malcolm?"

"I hope it's another survivor, sir," Malcolm said then scurried below to grab the mike, "Craig station rescue…come in please…this is the cutter *Largo*…repeat this is the cutter *Largo*…we have an emergency." He was going to add 'again' but stopped himself. It had been a hectic day.

"I'd be verra pleased, Sandy, if you'd radio for an ambulance." Tam broke in, his voice exhausted. "The woman is in need of one right quick."

"Malcolm's on it, Tam," Sandy called above the noise of both engines. "We're towing you in!"

Sandy threw a line and Hamish caught it handily. The cutter slowly towed Tam back into the harbour. By the time they got there a crowd of cheering fisherman waited on the pier.

A familiar police van sat at the top of the launching ramp, red light flashing. Beside it was an ambulance. Attendants, with a proper stretcher this time, stepped awkwardly down the sloping cobblestones of the broad harbour wall. They were accompanied by several fisher-men eager to lend a hand. Annie and Hamish were or-dered off the boat by a couple of burly characters Hamish thought he recognized. Nimble-footed, the men stepped aboard the *Molly Girl*, rolling in the tide. Katherine, still roped to the cabin door was up, out and on the stretcher as easily as any lobster creel they'd ever brought ashore.

Annie's father had a face like thunder as he approached.

"We found her at the cove, Daddy, on her boat. It was breaking up on the rocks. She could have died." Annie clutched her father's arm to steady herself.

"And what about you, Annie? Isn't once enough?"

Elbows of the crowd of pub onlookers jostled, interrupting.

"Is that Rory and Dugald?" Hamish whispered to Tam as they walked up the cobbled ramp.

"Right you are, lad, now watch this."

They were level with the *Gull and Spoon* now. The scary duo dashed inside and soon emerged with a glass in hand. They went over to the stretcher where Katherine lay, now awake apparently, and handed it to her. The attendant shook his head.

"What was in the glass?" Hamish asked fascinated.

"Brandy," said Tam, "for the survivor; it's tradition."

* * *

"I would never ha' believed it if I hadn'a seen it wi' me own eyes," Tam said spinning out the yarn. He was the man of the hour at the *Gull and Spoon*. His fellow fisherman crowded around to be entertained.

"Wee Annie stayed with the woman all afternoon keeping her alive. T'was a miracle she found her." Tam took another generous swig of his beer.

The barman, reached over to slap his back "Good job she thought o' you to help out, Tam."

"I'm telling you, Dugald, I would no' have done it for just any lass, but Annie, now, she's a brave one a' right. Then there's Hamish. I doubt he's been much at sea afore. Not too happy he was once the waves picked up."

"Must 'a been a right squeeze, the four o' you in your wee skiff!" laughed Alec.

"I left a lobster pot or two moored back at the cove, let me tell you. Not just the space, but the weight. Had a mind to tell young Hamish to walk home for all he was putting me through; nearly had a fit when I saw the woman."

"Could o' towed him back to harbour, behind ye like." The comment came from Rory.

"Aye, that would'a' been an idea!"

The party was picking up.

*   *   *

A bundle of bedraggled black fur sat on the back steps to greet Annie when she and her Dad got home.

"Bozz!" Annie cried scooping him up. "Where *have* you been?"

"Yeow?"

"I was so worried, Bozz," Annie nuzzled her face into his fur, "wandering off like that; very naughty, very naughty indeed."

"Indeed," her father's voice was sarcastic, "not so nice when you think you've lost something you love, is it?"

*   *   *

Molly and Aileen had been directed to manage dinner on their own and seemed happy to do so. No one in their right mind would have wanted to be within firing range of either of Annie's parents on this particular evening.

"Margaret, would the three of you rather talk this through on your own?" Gran began, unsteadily.

"Absolutely not, mother. You are in this as thick as Annie, though from what you've already told me my daughter did a bang-up job of leading you astray."

Annie's heart sank. She was really backed into a corner now not knowing which beans Gran had actually spilled and hoping to protect them both from the firestorm that was building. "I am so, so sorry. I know you must all be very angry with me."

"Angry! You must be joking," her father burst out. "Your mother and I are beyond angry. What you did bordered on madness. I shudder to think how it all *might* have played out." Her father shook his head and squeezed at his face with his hands.

Annie looked to Gran for a smile of understanding but it wasn't there. The old lady looked haggard, almost unwell, and Annie felt a cold chill of fear.

"So, dear girl," her father pressed on, holding Annie in an unforgiving stare, "are you going to supply us with some reason for your behavior?" Silence hung in the air around the table. The familiar clash of dishes faded into the background.

"I was looking for Bozz," Annie began then stepped out onto thinner ice. "You see, after he followed me down to the beach the other night I was afraid he might have drowned."

"As we did you," her mother shot back.

This was going to be even worse than Annie

realized. But how much should she tell them? She was mortified by their anger but was also afraid of their ridicule. "There was something else," she began again, choosing her words very carefully, "I had a model boat that I had fixed up for Moira, you see. I gave it to Hamish to test out the afternoon we were at Gran's, Mummy."

"I fail to see what this has to do with the situation at hand, Annie," her mother interrupted, "so you can forget about spinning another of your tales. I'm not as gullible as Gran you know."

Gran's head shot up, "Well, I never!"

Annie coughed and went on. "Hamish lost the boat, Mummy, and I was so upset. You see it was very special because I wanted to have it for Moira. When he didn't bring it back I went out at night to search for it."

Gran's unhappy eyes were riveted on Annie.

"And you think putting some amusement ahead of your life is a good idea?" You could cut the sarcasm in her father's voice with a knife.

If only he knew it was for Moira's life that she'd risked her own. But it was too much to try to explain and they were in no mood to understand. Even Gran must have had her doubts though she didn't say so then or now.

"But let's move along now. What about this more immediate business of being out at the cove; did you think your toy boat was there?" her mother's cutting tone made Annie cringe.

"Maybe," Annie said almost too softly to be heard.

"Oh, I haven't time for any more of this," said her mother with mounting impatience. "We are going around in circles."

"Plainly we are only hearing part of the story, Annie," her father put in. "But maybe this will do for now. We are all very tired. Your mother and I will talk further and decide what consequences you are going to be facing."

Then Gran spoke. "Don't either of you believe that what Annie did, no matter how reckless or difficult to justify in adult terms, has led to a wonderful outcome. A young woman's life has been saved. You can scarcely overlook that."

Annie watched her parents' faces and gradually their hard expressions softened a little. Gran had chosen her words well.

God bless, Gran.

*   *   *

The subject was dropped after that. Gran stayed on for a bite of supper then insisted on going home on foot.

"It's a braw evening, Margaret, and the walk will help me sleep. After a day like this I could do with a fine, long rest."

*   *   *

Unfortunately there were more angry words after Gran left. Annie was told she was seriously grounded. They hadn't said for how long and Annie didn't ask.

The 'sentence' was delivered and a peace, of sorts, restored so that Annie now sat propped up in bed with her parents for company.

"What'll happen to the wreck, Daddy?"she asked, taking a gulp of hot milk.

"I don't know." Her father's tone was gentler than she'd heard since her return home. "Depends on how bad the damage is. She certainly sounds pretty far gone from your description."

"What I don't understand, Sandy, is how the Coast Guard missed finding the boat."

"With all the weather we've been having, Margaret," he explained, "first the storm then all that fog, it's no surprise we missed the boat, especially one that'd been dismasted."

Annie leaned forward, "It would have been hard to see unless you went right in, like Tam did. And Hamish and I would never have seen it at all if we hadn't been at the top of the cliff."

"Don't remind me," said her father sharply. "I'm still having a very hard time casting you in the role of rescuer."

Annie backed down and took another sip from her mug. She had another urgent question but hesitated to ask it right then.

"What's buzzing round it that mind of yours now?" her mother asked. It was uncanny how she did that.

"I was just wondering," Annie began slowly, "how soon someone will be going out to the wreck; to check things over, I mean?"

"Malcolm and I will go tomorrow."

"Can I come?" Annie ventured.

Her father gave her a hard look.

"Won't you need me to show you where the wreck is?" Annie hoped he realized that, grounded on not.

"It would save some time, yes," her father conceded.

"And Hamish too; he found the cove the first time."

"Oh good lord, Annie, yes. Both of you can come," said her father, looking harassed.

Annie yawned and set her mug on the bedside table. "Thank you, Daddy."

"You must be exhausted, honey," he said a moment later. "Try to get some sleep now." He leaned forward and kissed her forehead.

"See you in the morning, Daddy."

"Goodnight, my impossible but daring daughter," her mother said with a rueful smile and a loving kiss. She tiptoed across the room and closed the bedroom door.

Bozz immediately jumped up on Annie's bed, "Yeow?"

Annie pulled her furry friend under the covers. "Dearest Bozz I missed you so much!"

Now if this amazing day had only ended with her finding *Bill* too it would have been almost perfect.

Chapter Twenty-Four

In the News

The kitchen was a much happier place next morning with everyone getting a huge kick out of the feature story in the local paper too. Sandy was trying to read it aloud to anyone who'd listen while the usual breakfast rush went on around him.

"Young Annie McLeod has done more than help the local Coast Guard locate a missing vessel, she has saved the life of its female skipper, Katherine Wakefield...That name," he mused. "I seem to remember...

Annie stopped him. "Not now, Daddy. Go on with the story."

"Yes, do please, Sandy."

"Aileen is that toast ready yet?" Molly called from the swing door to the dining room.

"Aye, and there's bacon in the oven for the guests at the window table."

"Hard for a fellow to get anyone's attention around here," Annie's dad complained shaking out the paper.

"I'm listening," said Aileen, laughing for a change.

"That's good." He continued, *'While out on some youthful exploration trip with her friend Hamish Findlay, the two discovered a recently wrecked boat in a hidden cove several miles up the coast toward St. Andrew's. Believing there may be injured crew aboard Annie insisted they check it out. It was a risky business climbing on a boat impaled on the rocks but Annie put her safety in second place.'*

"She's right brave our Annie is," said Aileen.

Nice of her thought Annie.

Annie's mum took a moment to check on the coffee, now bubbling up in the Kona on the gas stove then turned back to Sandy, "It's rather thrilling, isn't it; our daughter in the news."

"I'm going to need more of that bacon, Aileen!" called Molly sliding the last rashers onto a serving plate.

Sandy McLeod soldiered on, more loudly. *'She was also the one to remain with the injured woman keeping her warm, comfortable and hydrated until Hamish could return with assistance. When the Coast Guard was unavailable to help some fast thinking on Hamish's part allowed for a most unorthodox rescue. The local fishing community is thrilled to have Tam Dewart and his diminutive dory, 'Molly Girl', declared part of the rescue mission.'*

'Diminutive dory', lovely phrase that. But to continue: *'This life saving drama is testament to the bravery and ingenuity of youth and of Annie McLeod in particular. Rumor has it that there may be a substantial reward due.'* Well, isn't that Jock Harris all over again, Margaret? He just loves a story where he can show off a fancy turn of phrase."

"What's he mean about a 'substantial reward',

Daddy?" asked Annie scraping empty egg shells into the dust bin under the sink.

"I have no idea. Perhaps Mr. Wakefield said something to the press that I am unaware of."

"Then it is only a rumor; the reward part?" Annie asked again.

"I expect we'll find out soon enough, honey. Adam Wakefield wants me to get over to the cove right away to see what sort of state the vessel is in and let him know what I think." Her father's voice stopped and he slapped his leg. "This name Wakefield; It may just be a coincidence but..."

"Heavens dear, what is it?" Annie's mother set the fresh coffee on a tray for Molly.

"That name, Margaret... It was a Wakefield I met a couple of years back. He was at The Sailor's Exhibit in Dunadrin. Quite fascinated he was with the model boats. There were several of mine on display there but it was The *William Morr* he specially fancied. I expect it's still out there in my workroom, somewhere. I should go and take a look."

Annie hardly dared to breathe.

"And that's not all. It was the first model I had actually built from a detailed set of plans. It was for one of the courses I took in naval architecture. It was all down on paper before I even picked up my tools."

Annie felt the colour drain from her face.

"Honey," said her mother, "are you alright?"

"You look right pale," said Aileen.

"I, I'm fine." She looked straight at her father now. "Daddy what does this have to do with the boat at the cove?"

"Well, if it's not just a wild coincidence, and I'll know after we get down there and take a look, then it's just possible that these two boats are identical."

"I knew it!" Annie burst out then clapped her hand over her mouth.

"Sandy, that's incredible, but how?"

Molly set her tray down.

"Well, as I was saying, I had the *William Morr* model on display at the Sailor's Exhibit and it was Wakefield, of Wakefield Yachts no less, who wanted to buy my model and have one of his architects build a full size version as a gift for his daughter."

"And so you sold it to him?" asked Annie's Mum, tuning into the conversation again.

"No, darling, just the plans," he said rubbing his beard. "And you know what else? When Malcolm told me about the missing vessel I thought he called it *The Moore* but he must have said *The Morr*. So, Annie is right, maybe we have a match. I can hardly believe it."

"Then you never saw the boat after the Wakefield's had her built?" asked Annie.

"Incredibly, I didn't. The shipyard is on the west coast and not near here. I suppose I was just so busy with my studies and all the work moving here and then the renovations too that it never happened."

"But now you know we've *got* to save it, don't we?" Annie could barely contain her excitement.

"That's not my decision, honey. I have to take a look at her first and then tell Wakefield if it even makes sense to try to salvage her."

"So you'll be meeting him again, Sandy?" Annie's mother gave her husband a pointed stare.

Molly, smiling broadly, picked up the coffee tray and headed for the dining room.

"That has a happy ring to it, Sandy; the owner of Wakefield yachts."

"You're getting ahead of yourself, Margaret."

*   *   *

It was mid morning by the time they picked up Hamish and drove over to the station for Malcolm. Then they set off overland to Smuggler's Cove by jeep.

"Did you see the piece in this morning's papers?" Sandy asked as they bumped over the scrubby pastureland not much more comfortably than Annie and Hamish had on their bikes.

"Certainly did, Sandy. Quite the heroes, you two are," he said reaching out to give each a friendly slap on the hand.

"We are actually quite proud of our adventurers, *this time*," Sandy looked pointedly at his daughter. "Annie has more gumption than we gave her credit for. Looks as if she dragged *you* into the thick of it, right Hamish?"

"I was scared skinny about leaving Annie alone with Miss Wakefield!"

"I bet you were!" said Malcolm. "So tell us. How did you enjoy the trip on *Molly Girl*?"

Hamish was delighted for the chance to tell his story for a change.

"You should have seen Tam's face when we swam up to his boat!" Hamish began. Their ride was now punctuated with hoots and guffaws of laughter as well as bumps.

"And when we finally got the door secured across the gunnels Tam didn't say another word till we saw the *Largo* outside the harbour," Hamish said, winding up the story with a grin, "but then he didn't say much on the way out to the cove either!"

"Are we getting close, Hamish?" asked Annie's dad.

"It's just up there, sir." He pointed at the rise ahead.

Nearer the ridge they pulled over. Annie's bicycle was still lying on the grass where she'd left it the day before.

The wind blew in gusts as they crested the hilltop. They had to shout to be heard.

"Looks to be shifting a whole lot, Sandy!" Malcolm called out.

"Come on, let's get down there!" her father yelled back. Time was running out for the *William Morr* with every minute they delayed. "Coming, Annie?"

"Not yet. I should get my bike back in the jeep first." She stood on the grassy cliff edge and watched Hamish and the two men jump and run down the steep incline then stride across the beach. The bike was an excuse. Why had she asked to come? She couldn't go down there again.

*   *   *

"That's her all right; my *William Morr*," Sandy said, his words heavy with dismay.

"Sir?"

"That's my boat, Hamish. I know every inch of her."

"But how?"

"Later." Annie's Dad moved up across the rocks,

closer. "It's the hull that worries me most," he said turning to Malcolm. "Once they pull her off that hole in her will open up even more."

"That mast'll have to be removed first," added Malcolm his voice tight. "It'll tear the deck away left as it is. As God is my witness, Sandy, no matter how often I see a wreck up close, and I've seen a few in my day, I feel ill."

"But thank the Lord, Hamish, that you and Annie were able to get the woman off. I wouldn't want to be climbing up there today." Annie's Dad picked up a piece of line from the rocks and threw it in the water.

"Annie climbed up on that, sir, before it broke away," said Hamish.

Malcolm whistled. "Your girl has guts, Sandy, and then some."

They moved on in silence, running their hands over the parts they could reach, testing for soundness, Sandy making mental notes. The gaping hole really was the worst. They could see right inside.

Malcolm wandered back from the far side of the wreck shaking his head. "We might as well get back, Sandy. I think it's hopeless."

The gulls whirled overhead their cries like lost souls.

*   *   *

An older boy, maybe fifteen or sixteen, was leaning against the back door when Annie and her dad returned from Smuggler's Cove. He wore an ill fitting grey jersey with buttons missing over his rumpled woolen shorts. A large cardboard box stood on the step beside him and judging from his expression he had been waiting for some time.

He straightened up as soon as he saw them. "My name's Dugald McTavish. My da works at the *Gull and Spoon*," he began unhelpfully.

"What's this about then, Dugald?" asked Annie's Dad.

The boy cleared his throat. "This's for you, sir," he said picking up the box.

At that moment Bozz emerged from the house and wound himself around Annie's legs.

Annie scooped him up. Bozz purred.

Startled, Dugald looked at Bozz, recognition on his face. "Well I'll be! So this is *your* cat, miss? Mebbe it has something to do with it all, then."

"Something to do with what?" Annie couldn't tear her eyes away from the box.

Her dad opened the back door. "Perhaps you had best come in, lad. Take a seat and let's hear what you have to say. "Margaret, have you got a minute?"

"What is it Sandy?"

"We have a visitor with a box, Meg; thought you'd be interested. Annie and I certainly are."

The boy shuffled uncomfortably and placed the closed box on the kitchen floor beside his chair. Annie's mother sat beside him.

Molly and Aileen stood listening too, dish towels in hand.

"I was with my chums down at the place where your daughter," he hesitated, "where Annie was found t'other day. We were curious like, my chums were."

"Were you now?" said Annie's mum, an edge in her voice.

"We meant no harm, madam."

"And then?" her father asked.

"Well it was that strange, sir. After the police left and all, we were about to go too when we saw the cat. I know it was your daughter's cat now; I didn't then."

"Go on."

"Well it hung about like, then it walked down the rocks further to the sea."

"Bozz knew I'd been there," Annie's voice was faint.

Annie's parents exchanged anxious glances.

"But then the cat, it leaned over the water and put a paw in. I was that startled sir. I've not seen a cat do anything like that before."

"I dare say," said her Dad.

"But then it ran off, somewhere."

"He didn't come home," said Annie.

Dugald went on. "We didn't go back for a day or two, what with the storm and all, but then I got to wondering what it was would make a cat do that, so I went back on my own and there it was again; the cat I mean. Yesterday morning, it was, when the tide was out; after the fog lifted. I watched the cat for a wee while then it was off again. Only this time I walked over to where it'd been. I kneeled down and looked into the water, to be at cat height like, and it was then I saw it; the fishing net, and this."

Dugald raised the flaps on the box. "I came by yesterday but you were not home and I had to make sure I gave it to you, direct like. I've seen some of your models at the Sailor's Exhibit, sir. They are right beautiful," he said and extracted the very thing that Annie was praying for.

"So I was wondering sir; is this one of yours?" he said holding out the battered *William Morr*.

* * *

Dugald had barely closed the door behind him when Annie burst out, "Daddy, I can explain about *Bill*."

"What?"

"*Bill*, this model," she pointed at the box where the mangled *William Morr* was resting.

"You know about this!"

"I'm afraid I do. An awful lot, Daddy; and it's all my fault that he's wrecked because I was the one who took it."

"You took it? From my workshop?" Angry lines creased her father's brow.

"Annie, you *didn't*." Her mother sounded shocked too.

Annie squeezed her hands. "I knew you'd be upset, Daddy, probably more than upset, but it wasn't for me it was for… for someone else." She knew she wasn't making sense. "I thought *Bill* was lost forever and I was terrified for Moira and about what you'd say or do if you ever discovered he was missing," she rushed on. "I'd almost lost hope that someone could actually find *Bill* and bring him back after all that's happened. You see I'd looked everywhere myself…" Annie struggled to control the rush of emotions that overwhelmed her. "And now he's here, Daddy, and I'm just so happy; and so scared too." Her eyes looked up at him, imploring.

"So *this* is what you were looking for down by the sea the other night?"

Annie nodded.

Her father's eyes drilled into Annie's. "This is the 'toy' you had taken for Moira's amusement and have now destroyed?"

"Please, *please,* don't be angry, Daddy. I can explain; it was an accident; both times." Annie burst into tears.

Chapter Twenty-Five

Just Twenty-Four Hours

Annie's dad was poring over his desk at the coast guard station working on the possibilities for salvaging the *William Morr* when the phone rang. It was Adam Wakefield.

"What do you think, McLeod?" he asked the moment Sandy identified himself.

"Not good, sir. I would say if you don't get her off those rocks in the next twenty-four hours there won't be enough left to save."

"Really?" There was a rush of surprised breath on the line.

"It's pretty bad," Sandy continued. "I was about to put it in writing."

"Just twenty- four hours you said?" Wakefield's voice was cool and in control.

"But then maybe you have no interest in doing that, sir?"

"I do, I do. We can't just leave her there to break up.

202

Katherine would be devastated. Let's pull her in and take a closer look."

"Very well," Sandy agreed. "An assessment's best done on dry land anyway."

"Then you know what?" Wakefield cut in. "I'm not going to wait for your report. Let's just move her. I'll try to arrange for a barge and hauling equipment right away."

"I think we can help, there, sir. We've a company just a few miles up the coast that hauls wrecks. We've dealt with them before and they're reliable."

"McLeod, you're a good man. Handle this for me. I'll leave Glasgow this afternoon. I'll meet you at the harbour first thing in the morning. Can you arrange the salvage operation by then?"

"Shouldn't be a problem. Far as I know there's nothing else as urgent right now," said Sandy. "McGrath should put me at the head of the queue."

"Tomorrow, then McLeod."

"Tomorrow, sir." Annie's father heard the line go dead and he slowly replaced the receiver. He was playing his cards close to his chest, as the saying goes, because he hadn't told Wakefield that he had designed *The Morr*. He didn't think he could take the disappointment if it made no difference.

*   *   *

The operation was underway next morning. Hamish and Annie, her dad and Adam Wakefield stood together on the foredeck of *Largo*, now moored in the cove, watching McGrath at work. They'd decided on taking the cutter because it was faster *and more comfortable* than the trip over land and they had a far better view from *Largo's* deck than standing down on a rocky beach.

Annie and Hamish had never seen anything like it. Their front row 'seats' let them witness at close range just how complicated and time consuming a salvage operation could be. The mast was taken away first. The crew on the barge then started feeding huge leather straps under the hull to bear the weight of the boat. But the damage was so bad in places it was hard to decide where to position them. Each operator had a different idea and their opinions took time to be resolved. Finally the lines and pulleys were connected and they began painstakingly lifting the boat off the rocks.

"Easy! Easy!" a man in yellow slickers yelled up to the hoist operator, "this is no' Tam's wee dory ye're moving!"

Hamish laughed. "Have you seen *Molly Girl*?" he said to Adam Wakefield.

"No, but I'd love to."

"She is something else let me tell you, sir!"

"Then you must do that; when you come over to Glen Fellan. Katherine should be out of hospital by next week. I've asked Annie and her parents to come for a little celebration then. You'll come too, of course?"

They were interrupted by a loud shout. "Keep her o'er to starboard! I said *starboard*, you galloot! No' port!"

The *William Morr* was now suspended over the sea and every moment she hung there was agony to watch. She swayed a little, moved a little toward the barge, swayed a little more. It was worse than a high wire act at the circus.

"Why do you call the *William Morr*, 'she'?" Annie asked during a lull in the excitement.

"Tradition, Annie," Adam Wakefield called back. "No matter the name of a ship, or any floating craft in fact, she's aye a woman."

Her father smiled. "Always 'she'," he confirmed. "Sailors are very superstitious. It may have something to do with the dangers of the sea and their belief that the love of a woman, whether mother, sister or sweetheart, would be the way to keep them safe."

"I like that," said Annie.

"Sounds a bit sappy to me," Hamish said.

They were lowering the *William Morr* now, in slow motion, onto a huge trestle support, on board the waiting barge.

"That's called a 'cradle'," said Annie's dad.

"And that's some baby," Hamish laughed.

"Imagine if they'd had to do this on a stormy day," said Annie.

"Couldn't have," said her dad abruptly.

Every word from the crew echoed up from the cove. "Pay out that line! That's right… lower now. Mair line, now Jock, and lower her *all* the way now!"

"Where're they taking her?" asked Hamish.

"Down the coast a bit. There's an old boat yard there that's been out of operation since the war," explained Wakefield. "I'm having someone from my company take a look at her as soon as possible."

At last all the lines were secured across the barge decks. The *William Morr* was held in a tight embrace with the broken mast secured alongside.

"Slow ahead for'ard! Ease her out!" the captain called and the barge rounded slowly out from Smuggler's Cove.

Chapter Twenty-Six

Glenfellan

Hamish showed up at Annie's the following week wearing a shirt and tie, his unruly red hair, capless for a change, slicked down with something shiny.

"Don't say a word, Annie. It's my dad's hair cream and I smell like a girl."

Annie giggled.

"My Mum said I had to look presentable to meet the Wakefields."

"Oh, you look *very* presentable."

Annie's heart was bursting with possibilities for the day ahead made even better by the wonderful news that had arrived the night before. Aunt Grace had called to say that Moira was out of danger and was being discharged from hospital. The tests had come back negative. She did not have polio or infantile paralysis or whatever that wretched illness was called. It had been no more than a bad case of influenza. The doctors were now suggesting that a dose of fresh sea air would probably put everything right. And all this, Annie smiled just thinking about it, 'after' *Bill* had been returned.

* * *

The picture of the Wakefield estate Annie had in her mind didn't do it justice. Squashed into the back seat of their Hillman, she and Hamish craned their necks to see the full height of the wrought iron gates that swung open to greet them. Once through they followed a second road that wound its way past tall stands of arching beech and oak trees. Shards of sunlight splashed onto the car through the branches like a display of daylight fireworks.

"Wow!" said Annie.

"Double wow," said Hamish

Where the canopy of trees ended the road opened out onto a circular drive that skirted a vast central lawn. Daddy geared down and the engine raced a little.

"I'm going to drive right up to the front door. I suppose we shall be met there. Or should I look for the tradesman's entrance?" her father joked.

As they drew up to the covered portico Annie gulped.

A uniformed gentleman with a crest on his jacket stood at the entrance as the car pulled up. The instant the Hillman stopped he walked toward the passenger door and swung it open.

"Mrs. McLeod, welcome to Glen Fellan." He reached out and took her mother's arm.

"Mr. McLeod, you may leave the car here. Someone will park it for you."

Annie and Hamish were standing on the pebbled
driveway when Katherine Wakefield appeared at
the front door. She sat in a wheelchair with her legs
propped out in front. She waved her arms in greeting.

"Annie, how wonderful to see you again and Mr.
and Mrs. McLeod too."

"Please, call me Sandy," Annie's father insisted,
running up the steps, "and this is my wife, Margaret."

"I'm delighted to meet you." Katherine took Annie's
mother's hand and held it a moment before taking her
father's.

"And this is Hamish," said Annie making her in-
troduction as rehearsed. "Hamish I would like you to
meet Katherine."

"Very pleased to meet you, Miss Wakefield,"
Hamish managed without a stumble.

"Hamish, my other saviour!" Katherine laughed.
But it was Annie her eyes went back to.

"That's fine Dobson, I will see them in." Katherine
addressed the liveried servant who had met them. She
swiveled her chair in a half circle. "My father is on
the telephone," she said and wheeled off into a huge
lounge. "Another call from his firm in Glasgow I expect. He'll join us momentarily, I'm sure."

On cue, Adam Wakefield came hurrying down the
hallway and through the French doors.

"My apologies; business. I just can't get away from
it enough to enjoy family and friends."

"Papa," Katherine took Annie's mother's arm, "this
is Margaret McLeod."

"Mother to our famous Annie," said Adam
Wakefield, his eyes twinkling then he turned to Sandy

and shook his hand warmly. "Good to have you here, my man."

"The pleasure is mine, sir."

Katherine was in her element surrounded by visitors. "And I know you've already met our two young heroes, Papa, but *I've* had to wait till now to meet this young man properly. Dear Hamish," she said, reaching out to him, "I don't suppose you would permit me a hug, would you?"

Hamish blushed to the roots of his shining red hair.

*   *   *

Annie felt as though she had come home. She knew it was far grander than any she was ever likely to live in but that didn't seem to matter. She and her parents were obviously as welcome as any family member could be. Perhaps, one day soon, Gran could meet them too.

"First," began Adam Wakefield before anyone had a chance to sit down in the splendid lounge, "let me officially welcome all of you to Glen Fellan. My daughter and I are delighted to have you with us. I need not tell you what a very different event would have been taking place had not Annie and Hamish chosen to cycle out to Smuggler's Cove a week ago."

Annie's mother squeezed her husband's hand and smiled at her daughter then at Hamish too. Katherine bent her head over her lap for a moment then looked up to meet the gaze of each person in the room.

"My daughter and I cannot begin to express our gratitude," Wakefield continued. "Some things are beyond words but please know that each of you have a place in our hearts for the rest of our lives."

"Oh, Papa." Katherine appeared to be on the edge of tears along with just about everyone in the room.

Wakefield then walked round the room and solemnly shook the hand of each guest while two black suited waiters entered the room bearing trays of drinks along with some tiny portions of scrumptious-looking food.

Wakefield turned to his guests again, "And now, may I propose a toast or two." Glasses of something bubbly were presented to everyone.

"First to Annie, probably one of the bravest young girls I have known."

"To Annie!" responded everyone.

"And to Hamish for his quick thinking and determination."

"To Hamish!"

"And *Molly Girl*," Hamish added making everyone laugh to cover his embarrassment.

"And to some very fine parents, Margaret and Sandy McLeod, not to mention Jean and David Findlay who, unfortunately, were not able to join us today," Katherine added with feeling.

Hamish blushed again.

"*For they are jolly good fellows!*" sang Annie, raising her glass.

"Now, please everyone, let's enjoy a bite before we move on to further business," Adam Wakefield invited, extending his arms.

The delicious appetizers were passed around. Annie watched her mother making mental notes and wondered which of the Wakefield specialties might be served at *Lin Cove* very soon. Hamish put something on his plate every time it was offered.

By now her father had started talking to Adam Wakefield leaving her mother and Katherine to find a subject of their own. Hamish chose a chair beside the men. Annie did too.

"So you'll have had time to go over my report by now," said Annie's father setting down his plate. "Have you decided what you want to do with the *William Morr*?"

"I don't know quite how to say this McLeod, but *my* man is telling me that the yacht is too far gone to rebuild."

You could have heard a pin drop. Mrs. McLeod and Katherine looked over in concern. Annie felt her stomach lurch.

"Really," her father managed.

Annie saw his face fall. Hamish stopped chewing and just stared.

"Well," said Wakefield after an uncomfortable silence, "that seems to have hit all of you rather hard."

"It has," Annie's dad said, "and, if you don't mind, I would like to tell you why, sir."

"Please," Adam Wakefield refilled his glass, "please go on."

"Well here it is. It seems you did not recognize me with my beard, sir, not to mention that it's *has* been a couple of years as well since we first met."

"It has?" Wakefield looked puzzled.

Hamish sat on the edge of his chair. It was the explanation he'd been waiting for. Annie knew what was coming but somehow the joy had been knocked right out of it.

"It was at the Sailor's Exhibit in Dunadrin a couple of years ago," Annie's father continued. "You wanted to buy one of my model boats. I tried to explain that they were not for sale but I was flattered because the model was one of my own, and a fairly decent one at that. I had built it according to some very detailed plans I developed."

"I had no idea you were *that* McLeod!"

"You stayed at the exhibit for quite a while examining the models. In the end you came back and offered me an outrageously high sum for mine," Annie's father cleared his throat; a habit he had when he felt embarrassed. "You said you wanted to have a boat built just like it for your daughter. Knowing how difficult that would be I offered to sell you a set of my drawings instead. I gather now that the builder was you."

"Wow!" Hamish ran his hands through his hair.

Adam was putting the pieces together too, "You used the name Alexander on your plans, didn't you?"

"I did, yes. And, of course you now know, that it was my *William Morr* that you had built. You even asked if I would mind if you retained the name. I was delighted because now the *Morr* would become the full scale boat I had intended it to be. You see I had named it after a dear friend I served with during the war. Had he lived he would have been even more thrilled than I to be at sea again."

"Good lord! Now I can see why this means so much to you."

"Mr. Wakefield," said Annie her mouth trembling.

"My Daddy can fix anything, honestly he can. Please let him try?"

"Honey, we've been through all this," her father said quietly, but firmly. "You knew before we came here that the decision was not ours to make." Then he turned to Wakefield. "I'm sorry, sir, my daughter seems to have developed a rather close attachment to your boat; as we all have."

Katherine rolled her wheel chair over to her father's side. "Papa, maybe we should reconsider. I can't bear to see Annie so distraught after all she has done for us."

Adam Wakefield paced back and forth then stood with his back to the fireplace. Some agonizing moments passed before he spoke again. "I think then, McLeod," he said at last, "this may be one of those times when a wise business decision may not the *right* decision." He took a swallow from his glass. "Clearly we would not even be having this conversation today if not for Annie and Hamish."

After another pause Annie's father asked, "Then this decision to scrap her is not final?"

"Perhaps not," Wakefield replied. "I did say, after all, that it was my *assessor's opinion*, not mine. He is a shrewd individual and very concerned with the Wakefield Yachts' bottom line."

"Then there is room for negotiation here?" Annie's father looked suddenly hopeful.

Annie fidgeted. She understood the general drift of the conversation but not the actual words.

"What are you suggesting, McLeod?"

"That perhaps you might consider my having a

hand in the reconstruction? It might be less expensive that way," Annie's father offered.

"Sandy," said Annie's mother, aghast, "when could you *possibly* take on such a project?"

"But it couldn't be right away, sir," Annie's dad looked straight at Adam Wakefield, "you see my wife and I run a summer hotel and I have obligations with the Coast Guard. I also have a thesis to finish at university."

Annie's heart did another flip.

"You *are* a busy man, Alexander. And this thesis you referred to. It has rather a lot to do with boats, hasn't it?"

"As a matter of fact I am less than a year away from a post graduate degree in naval architecture."

"Well, why didn't you say so? That's very interesting; very interesting indeed. The fact is, my company is about to expand. We are planning to set up a new yard on the east coast; right where the *William Morr* is sitting at this moment if you can believe it."

Annie held her breath. They were so close. Did Mr. Wakefield understand what Annie's father had *not* said; that it was all about money again; money that they didn't have?

Her father coughed. Annie knew he was on edge too.

"Then how does this sound?" Adam Wakefield's face grew flushed as he spoke. His hand was resting on Katherine's shoulder. "You come and work for me; right now. You can start with the restoration of the much loved *William Morr*. Once that's out of the way the new yard should be in full operation. Following that

McLeod, if all goes according to plan, you should have completed your studies and can take over as head of my design team. We have plenty of prospective clients just waiting to do business with us."

Annie's mouth dropped open. Her mother stared at Wakefield then looked down at her hands; waiting.

"It sounds wonderful, sir," her father's voice shook with emotion. "But I will have to make arrangements; the hotel; my wife can't manage on her own."

"For heaven's sake, darling," came the swift interruption, "I'll hire someone to do the things you've been doing."

"And the Coast Guard?"

Annie thought she would go mad with impatience.

"Sandy," said Margaret McLeod sounding almost as exasperated as Annie felt, "they'll find someone else, and when you've finished studying you can go back; as a volunteer if you want to!"

"I suppose I could; yes," he admitted.

"Then we have an agreement, McLeod?"

There were no uncomfortable pauses this time. "We do indeed, sir," said Annie's dad, the smile on his face growing as the two men shook hands and clapped each other on the back.

"Now, that you two have settled the business side," Katherine brought her chair forward again, "I would like to add something, Papa."

Adam Wakefield nodded.

"This is for my Annie and *her* papa," she said her warm gaze taking in Annie and her father. "When the *William Morr* is in shape again my plan is to come back and sail for a few weeks each summer. I promised *my*

Papa that." Her eyes shone. "But most of the time it will be here for you both to take care of and sail whenever you like."

And for the second time that morning you could have head a pin drop.

Annie blinked back tears. Not in her wildest dreams could anything have been more perfect but before she could think of a word to say the glass doors at the far end of the lounge opened. Piano music drifted into the room, as softly as moonlight, Annie thought. Her father's hand slipped into hers.

"Now if you would all come this way," said Adam Wakefield, "I do believe lunch is served."

Epilogue

Now there is the moonlight on the bay; the silver waves shimmer against the peaceful murmur of the tide. Annie stands at the top of the brae holding the hand of a small girl in pajamas.

"Isn't it beautiful?"

Moira looks up at her. She holds a model boat in her hands. It's scratched still and the mast looks mended.

"Can we sail Bill again tomorrow?"

"Of course."

"I'll pick a safe pool, Annie. We have to be extra careful 'cause he's getting old, you know."

* * *

Annie stares at her reflection in the mirror, at her blue blazer with the St. Andrew's Academy crest buttoned smartly over a tartan skirt. Bozz is curled up on her bed watching as she stuffs a copy of <u>Prince Caspian</u> with a bookmark note into her new schoolbag.

"I'm not going far… I'll be home every weekend."

Bozz jumps onto the carpet and winds his way around her legs.

"Are you ready, honey?" her father's voice comes from the hall below.

"Coming!"

*   *   *

Out on the bay a boat tacks by. Annie is at the helm with Katherine beside her watching the sails, releasing or tightening a sheet. There is easy conversation, gestures and nods. Hamish rides the bucking bow pulpit his legs skimming in and out of the surf below.

"That's the May Island," he calls back to them and points to a triangle of land pushing up from the sea to starboard.

From the cockpit the two wave to him shielding their eyes. The sun makes the sea glisten, the gulls swoop, diving near the fishing boats out for the afternoon catch.

*   *   *

And everything now is because of then.

A Letter from the Author

To my young readers:

When I was a child I built a boat, a simple craft much like the one that Annie made and discarded. I sailed it in the rock pools, probably losing it after a time, but it stayed in my memory.

My parents bought a house by the sea and turned it into a summer hotel. My mother, father and I all slept in whatever parts of the big house had not been booked for guests; a work shed in the back garden, a storage area off the kitchen. My mother, ever strong in time of hardship, turned it into a sort of camping adventure.

I did leave the private school I attended with my "well to do friends" and I did go instead to one filled with the children of the fisher folk and local merchants. I was very unhappy in that school, not because of my classmates but because the headmaster who was my teacher did not like children and he was unkind and his lessons were some of the dullest I could imagine. The only good thing about being in his class was it drove me to read everything I could get my hands on to escape the tedium of his classes.

Tam Dewart has a different name in my story but he was real. We used to see his tiny fishing boat out on the bay in any weather and wondered at the chances he took to fill his lobster traps.

The moon on the sea a night was a glory. The bay was like a gigantic bowl holding a treasure just for us. My mother and I would stand on the roadway, or the front garden, or by the window and gaze "till we lost our senses".

And pipe bands were magic too, like a whole throng of Pied Pipers they were. Any child, and especially me, would follow wherever they led, over streets or braes or sands, completely enthralled by the heavenly din they made.

Like Annie I was a lonely child, my friends always miles away re-grouped by their parents in distant places. My two brothers, 10 and 12 years older, were away at boarding school, and my parents, like many in the years following the war struggling to make ends meet, worked long hours and had little time to amuse their young daughter. Instead they gave me freedom.

And I confess I was a night wanderer. I have no crisp recollections of this, just a general feeling of delight at the darkness and the starlight and pull of the beach where my steps were taking me. I believe I was very young when I did this and it terrified my mother.

You see, in Scotland, the sun sets very late in the summertime. It was hard lying in bed in total daylight hearing the world going on around me and not be part of it. So once darkness came it was marvellous. It held secrets and possibilities and I wanted to know them all. And the sailing? It never happened in Crail, where my story is set, but rather years later when I married a man crazy about the sea. He taught me all about the boats he loved. We sailed the Great Lakes and the Eastern seaboard of the United States and places in the Caribbean too. Then once, when on holiday in Scotland and in the company of a dear friend, Sandy, we sailed where "Annie" did. Maybe that was the connection.

Anyway fiction is a funny thing. It picks its way through all sorts of memories and imaginings until it comes up with a story. It is a journey for the writer as much as for the reader and <u>Shire Summer</u> is mine.

Noelle Jack

Glossary of Scots Words

1. *Awa'*: away
2. *Aye*: always
3. *Brae*: sloping hill often covered in grass or heather
4. *Canna*: Cannot
5. *Chill*: cold
6. *Creel*: pot for trapping lobster
7. *Didn'a*: didn't
8. *Hersel'*: short for herself
9. *Lad or Laddie*: young boy
10. *Lass or lassie*: young girl
11. *Muckle*: a whole lot
12. *Neuk*: corner or nook
13. *Och aye*: Oh yes
14. *Rile*: upset
15. *Tak*: take
16. *The gither*: together
17. *Twa*: two
18. *Verra*: very
19. *Wee*: young
20. *Wi'*: short for with
21. *Ye*: you

Glossary of Sailing Words

1. *Berth:* bed or bench seat
2. *Boom:* heavy horizontal pole to which the bottom of a sail is attached
3. *Bulkhead:* the cabin wall
4. *Chart:* map of any body of water
5. *Chart table:* desk for working on charts
6. *Cockpit:* open steering section of a boat
7. *Companionway:* set of steps leading down into a boat
8. *Cutter:* small, fast boat often used for rescue
9. *Drop board:* board used to close off the companionway
10. *Fathom:* six feet
11. *Galley:* on board kitchen
12. *Gunnels:* top edges of the side of a boat
13. *Hoist:* raise
14. *Hull:* the side of a boat
15. *Keel:* board running downward from the centre of the hull to hold a boat stable
16. *Locker:* enclosed storage space on board
17. *Lifelines:* lines attached to stanchions to prevent falling overboard
18. *Maiden voyage:* first voyage
19. *Marker buoys:* anchored floats placed to direct boat traffic
20. *Mast:* Vertical pole that holds a raised sail

21. *Mooring:* floating buoy anchored near the shoreline where a boat can tie up
22. *Port:* left hand side
23. *Porthole:* round windows on board ship
24. *Rudder:* a flat board hinged at the stern used for steering
25. *Seaworthy:* built to withstand being at sea
26. *Sheet:* length of rope used to control sail position
27. *Stanchions:* upright supports for lifelines
28. *Starboard:* right hand side
29. *Stern:* back end of a boat
30. *Tack:* any change of direction at sea
31. *Tiller:* handle used to steer a boat
32. *Wake:* waves caused by a boat's bow or following off the stern
33. Winch: a rotating drum around which a line can be wound making it easier to pull

Bibliography of Quotations

P. 4 Chapter 1: "The Lady of the Lake" Sir Walter Scott

P. 104 Chapter 13: "Eriskay Love Lilt" Gaelic Folk Song

P. 121 Chapter 15: "The Old Sailor" from <u>Now We Are Six</u>, A.A. Milne

CPSIA information can be obtained
at www.ICGtesting.com
Printed in the USA
LVOW10s1820060817
544039LV00001B/15/P